ERNEST HAYCOX has long been considered
the unquestioned master of novels of the West.
His virile, exciting books brought him world-
wide fame, and made him one of the bestsell-
ing authors of all time.

HEAD OF THE MOUNTAIN is a masterful
story of two men, best friends, who must ride
to a bloody confrontation on a cold and star-
less night. At the Head of the Mountain, their
trials would cross, and for one of them the trail
would end. . . .

Ernest Haycox

Ⓢ Signet Brand Western

Exciting SIGNET Westerns by Ernest Haycox

Head
of
the
Mountain

by
ERNEST HAYCOX

Ⓢ
A SIGNET BOOK
NEW AMERICAN LIBRARY
TIMES MIRROR

COPYRIGHT © 1950-51, ERNEST HAYCOX

Originally published by *Esquire* Magazine

All rights reserved. For information address
The New American Library, Inc.

Published by arrangement with Jill Marie Haycox

SIGNET TRADEMARK REG. U.S. PAT. OFF. AND FOREIGN COUNTRIES
REGISTERED TRADEMARK—MARCA REGISTRADA
HECHO EN CHICAGO, U.S.A.

SIGNET, SIGNET CLASSICS, MENTOR, PLUME, MERIDIAN AND NAL
BOOKS *are published by The New American Library, Inc.,*
1633 Broadway, New York, New York 10019

FIRST SIGNET PRINTING, MARCH, 1978

3   4   5   6   7   8   9   10   11

PRINTED IN THE UNITED STATES OF AMERICA

PART
I

****

At the upper deck's railing Hugh Rawson watched the *Annie Conser*'s bow swing shoreward to search for Klickitat's landing stage. An ink-dense bluff rose behind the river, crowding the town into a single street whose lights lay out upon the water like the pickets of a yellow fence. Against the night's enameled black, star masses made their foamy glittering and the clear winds of spring blew lightly in from the empty reaches of Eastern Oregon. In Portland, where he had spent a month abed, the climate was a heavier and a sleepier thing; this mild air blowing against him was the fragrant breath of a woman gladly whispering him home.

Rawson lifted his carpetbag and took the forward stairs in a sidewise manner to protect a left leg not yet dependable. He moved ashore with this cautiousness, but in a moment his hustling habit got the better of him and he

3

put out a hand to make his way through the crowd toward the Klickitat House standing fifty feet from the river. He signed the register and went up the stairs and along a dim hall to a room. There, he removed coat and shirt, unbuckled the money belt around his hips, washed away the day's dirt, and dressed again. His skin had the olive tint of an active man too long indoors; his mouth was broad with small creases across its center meatiness, his nose was heavy, his cheekbones were flat and high. His face needed filling out and in fact he needed twenty more pounds all about his body to bring him back to the hundred and eighty pounds he had been. When he turned to the bed, he placed too much weight on his left leg and woke its unhealed nerves. He murmured, "Dammit," and drew his .44 with its holder and belt from the carpetbag, but he laid it aside while he rummaged the bag for a derringer. Cinching the money belt beneath his coat, he turned to the lobby.

Both lobby and bar of the Klickitat were crowded. Klickitat was a depot town; the boxes and barrels and bales of merchandise dropped by steamboat at the landing were picked up and carried on, eastward and southeastward, to the mining camps far beyond the Snake, along the Powder and the Malheur, into Boise Basin, over flinty hills and through colored gorges into Central Oregon, to solitary ranches on the high desert, to prospectors' settlements ephemerally lodged beside the gravelly bars of the John Day.

A denied appetite came powerfully upon him and the rear view of a familiar figure at the bar—a tremendously upholstered shape within a shabby blue suit tailored like a square tent—drew him forward. He created a place at the bar by shouldering Jake Mulvey into a smaller area.

"Get my letter?"

"I did," said Mulvey, and used a finger to catch the barkeep's eye. He smiled then; his mouth was benign and small and bride-red behind the ragged screening of a mustache. He was at least fifty-five, yet youngness seemed to have been permanently caught within the preservative lard which padded him head and foot. He looked at Rawson's leg.

"You're pushin' that too soon. You need a lot of feedin'. How."

They drank and crossed the lobby to the dining room. Rawson saw an empty table at a far corner; half over the room he heard his name called and swung to catch sight of George von Stern at another table—von Stern and Evelyn. He said to Mulvey, "Go on, I'll be with you in a second," and made his way toward these two. Von Stern got up and reached for Hugh's hand, and shook it thoroughly.

"Hughie, glad to see you—glad to. You all right?"

"Will be."

Evelyn said, "Don't ignore me."

The room's lamplight broke into brilliant splinters against her eyes. Her hand closed firmly around his hand and her glance searched him with a warming curiosity. Her lips were plush cushions against her skin, placid but falsely so, for she was not a placid woman. A yellow hat lay on hair which was the lightest possible brown, and her dress was a rusty gold, if gold could rust, the upper part of it cleverly broken and reshaped, she being the dressmaker. She was a large girl with a pleasant composure, but a contradictory vigor sparkled in her eyes and around her mouth a restless charm fugitively hovered, waiting escape. She was a light-loving woman, not calm, not cool; variety pleased her— the unexpected changes and contrasts which variety brought.

"Your friends," she said, "intended to make a party and come to Portland to see you, but the road out of Ophir's been so terrible." She drew her hand away; her interest hung on. "Eat with us."

"Business with Mulvey."

"It's a fool question," said von Stern, "but have you got a notion who shot you off the seat?"

Rawson swung his body back and forth.

"Listen. Hear the hip joint squeak? When I'm driving I won't know whether it's the coach rattling or me."

He smiled at Evelyn and he brought her smile back. He watched it grow and hold steady, and he tilted his head and seemed to observe it from a distance; then he made a motion with his hand and turned away. Evelyn watched him go between the crowded tables, slightly limping, now and then touching a table to steady himself.

She said, "If that's permanent I'll never again think there's anything kind in this world." She said it with a force that brought von Stern's glance to her. He said, "I thought this might sober him up. It didn't. He doesn't give a damn about anything."

The girl drew her glance from Rawson; she placed her hands on the table and tipped her head. "Oh no," she said, the words feathersoft, "he's changed. George, who'd hate him enough to shoot him while he was driving? He doesn't have that kind of enemies."

"They were after the express box."

"Could it have been a Piute?"

"An Indian's not interested in gold."

"Gold's a terrible thing," she said.

The color of von Stern's eyes, a thick coffee brown, was a rich mud behind which his emotions lay well covered; even when they reached surface they were never entirely free from a certain hint of reserve. He had a grave and coppery face, he was rawboned and strong-muscled with handsome and curled black hair always a little tumbled about his head, and he dressed himself carefully and kept himself shaved and groomed; a diamond ring, the great stone held in a gold snake's-mouth mounting, circled the index finger of his left hand. Softly speaking, he turned the diamond from side to side, watching the imprisoned flame flash. "Gold can do anything, and men will do anything for it. Greatest creator—greatest destroyer. I know of nothing with its power, and power's what we all want."

Rawson said, "I'll ride to Head of the Mountain and take the reins as before."

"Lay around a couple of weeks in Ophir and feed up," said Mulvey.

"I'm going after that fellow."

"It was six weeks ago and the country's full of drifters and there'd be no trace, unless you know who did it."

"I never saw him. He was behind a tree when he fired."

"Maybe he meant to fire a warning shot and hit you by mistake."

"At twenty feet? Nobody can shoot that poor. And if it was just the express box he wanted, he'd not shoot the driver and stampede the coach to hell and gone down the road. Maybe he wanted the box, but he wanted to kill me first. We'll be carrying a lot of dust out of Ophir this year. He'll try again —same idea as he had before—and I'll be on the box. Unless I catch him, he'll catch me."

"Rough game," said Mulvey.

Rawson used a thumbnail to scratch lines back and forth upon the tablecloth, closely watching the traveling of his hand and searching for a thought that would stand fast long enough to be captured by words. He was twenty-five, yet his face was the sort that experience did not edge or harden and his eyes, exceedingly blue, were tranquil. He shook his head. "This man's a pair of red eyes watching me from the brush. He missed once, but he's prowling and he'll try again. He's the same as telling me I'm not bright enough to stay alive. I'm interested."

"You stayed in bed too long and thought too damned much. You swallowed the hook. Wait till marbles start rollin' around your belly and your eyeballs feel full of pitch and needles."

"I'll take back the run from Bart Lennon," said Rawson, "but I'd like to use him for relief man when I want to prowl."

"That's all right," said Mulvey. He sat back in the chair, finger tips making a tepee before his eyes. He sighted across the finger tips to Rawson. "Couple years ago we never had much trouble, maybe a holdup or two, but nothing to worry about. I see it getting worse. It's the old story. Soon as a camp shows up rich the bad ones come from everywhere and the small crooks get together and pretty soon you've got a gang with some smart fellow running it. I think that's what we've got."

Leaving the dining room, Rawson noted that Evelyn and von Stern had already gone. Mulvey said, "I'll see you in the morning," and crossed the lobby while Rawson returned to the bar to buy himself a supply of cigars. He lighted one and left the bar, intending to settle his supper with a stroll along the town's main street. Passing the parlor he looked in and saw Evelyn Harvey there, her face to the lobby; she was alone.

He removed the cigar when he went in, holding it cupped in his hand; he looked down and noticed the uncertainty around her mouth. She made a small gesture and he settled himself and swung to face her, and at that moment a sensation went through him, as leaves would be lifted by a spiraling wind. She said, "I thought it would be nice to get out of Ophir for a bit. George had to make a trip so I just came along. But three days around here's enough. I'll be glad to get back."

He stared at his cigar. A month in bed had lightened his hands and had softened the calluses across his palms. It was clear that she wanted him to know, as soon as possible, why she and George were in town together. He raised his head and noticed how carefully she watched his face. He nodded. It surprised him that she felt it important to explain anything to him; she was old enough to run her own life.

She pointed to the cigar. "You want to smoke that thing. Let's walk." She took his arm and they passed into a street speckled with yellow lamplight. He looked at her, his smile coming through the spotty shadows. "Things been all right with you during the last month?"

"Yes," she said, "and it's nice you're interested. Wait a moment."

She turned into a store. He thrust his hands into his pockets and laid a shoulder against the doorsill, watching the inside scene. The lights of the store, striking her bronze dress built up a sparkling glow around her. She made her purchases and came out and took his arm. "Night's so lovely," she murmured, accommodating her pace to his steady stepping. They followed this street until the shop lights and the rough sounds of the town dropped back and the shadows of outlying sheds came upon them, the streets becoming a road whose ruts were deep as plow furrows.

"Pain's an awful thing," she said.

"After it goes away a curtain comes down and you can't bring back how bad it was. Otherwise we'd all be cowards."

"It leaves something behind. Your voice isn't the same. Neither's your smile."

11

"That's from lying in bed thinking too much. How's everybody? How's Ad Carrico?"

"Somebody's got to talk to him."

"That again? Well, it's Easterline's wife, not mine."

"It's sad. Sad for all of them."

"I don't know who's wrong there, Ad or Beth Easterline."

"I'm not talking about anybody being wrong."

They turned and walked back toward the beginning of the sidewalk and the first muddy stain of the town lamps. He halted and swung her around, her arrested body becoming a slight weight pushing against his hand. She was still, and smiling, and watchful. "Somebody's got to be wrong," he said.

"She made a bad bargain with Easterline and you think she should keep it. That's the wise thing, but she won't be wise. She knows it can't last, for Ad will be transferred someday, but it's like dying—she won't die till she must."

"If it's that serious," he said dryly, "maybe they'd better skip the country together."

"He'd ruin his career as an Army officer no matter how they worked it out."

He reached out with his other hand and now held her arms, trying to catch sight of her expression through the shadows, still receiving the mild inward insistence of her body. He dropped his hands and saw her check herself and heard the quick trembling of laughter in her throat. He laid his arms around her and she came in at once, lifting her head until he saw the distinctness of her smile; laughter seemed to bubble through her when he kissed her, her palms lodged lightly on his shoulders and her mouth met his and remained a moment and then fell away. She turned him and walked on with him into the clearer glowing of the house lights. "Welcome home, Hughie."

Later, alone in her room, she faced herself at the dresser's mirror; she put her hands on the dresser top, bent forward, and watched her features come back to her. Her lips were heavier, they were like sponges slowly being saturated; her face was alive, not simply pleasant but sharpened as though a stinging air had touched it; the pupils of her eyes were large and had a heavy glow in them. That was the face of a woman who had been roused too much, who hoped for too much. He had no idea what he had done to her; at this moment he was no doubt at the bar, amiably wasting his time with other men, the scene forgotten.

But she couldn't blame him for not knowing something she herself hadn't known. Coming to Ophir the year before, she had met him and had liked him, yet had not considered him to be more than a careless, good-looking young man contented with his job. The rest of it had grown without her knowledge until the time of his accident. That, and his ab-

sence, had shocked her; the sight of him walking into the dining room had made a greater
effect on her than she thought possible, and
the fact that she deliberately waited for him
in the hotel parlor was a warning that something had happened to her.

She swung from the mirror, restless and
not at all happy. This was too uncertain; it
was bound to hurt. For, looking at von Stern's
friendship with her and her acceptance of it,
Rawson had acquired a certain wonder con-
cerning her. He was courteous, but she had
felt its presence.

She moved to the window to let in night's
cool sweet air and, curious about all things,
watched the night marshal trudge along the
block and turn the corner. At that corner
George von Stern stood before a little man
who talked steadily, von Stern listening with
an occasional prompting nod. A thousand
times in Ophir she had seen him in that atti-
tude, dredging men for what they knew, and
as he repeated this scene she saw some small
new thing to push her closer to a final judgment of him. The solid strength which had
originally attracted her was, after better
knowledge of him, something else; and out
of the quiet places of his nature once lending
him a maturity and a mystery, came now the
queer current of hidden thoughts which
troubled her. She had liked him for his gal-
lantry, his knowledge of the world, and his

understanding of her, and it was a sad thing to see that go. He had changed, and so had she; and so had Rawson. Nothing remained the same.

Shaved and fed and cheerful, and a cigar fragrant between his teeth, Rawson stepped into a chilled bright morning to find the stage at the door of the Klickitat House, a shaken Concord coach hitched to four half-wild horses surging against the harness. On the driver's seat, Barney Rheinmiller held them in check with the reins. Barney was a Dutchman with lumpy shoulders, stone grey eyes, and a square face which had no more animation than tanned leather. Sixty miles of road between Klickitat and Head of the Mountain was a phenomenally exact picture in his mind, every bend and grade and chuckhole and draw, and in the blackest night he read the road shadows as other men read a printed page. He grinned down at Rawson.

"Got a hole in your head so you come back to drivin'. Where's the passengers?"

They came from the hotel—a drummer from Portland, Ack Trubo who was a cattleman in Skull Valley, von Stern and Evelyn. The other passengers entered the coach and Rawson climbed to the high seat. Rheinmiller threw off the brakes and issued a rough shout which exploded the horses into an immediate rushing run down the street; the road bent around a corner—which the coach took with a violent careening—and climbed the face of the bluff behind town.

Half an hour later the road reached the rim of the high country and put gorge and river behind. Southward a seemingly unbroken sagebrush plain rolled mile on mile toward the charcoal streak of mountains, and across this the road pressed, two ruts furrowed foot deep in an ash-light soil. The bright sun sailed up, sucking away the morning's chill, and a lightly variable wind blew.

"Damned fine day," said Rheinmiller.

"Any day's fine if you can stand up to see it," said Rawson.

Rheinmiller sat in loose disregard for the constant careening of the coach on its fore and aft straps; he cursed the individual horses conversationally and kept them at a steady eight miles an hour through the wriggling ruts. Rawson eased himself on a seat which for him, after a month in bed, was hard as stone. The stage, grumbling on at its maintained pace, wrote a straight line of dust through the sunlight, it hanging motionless as far as the eye reached. At Bird's, where the horses were changed, the last of the settled country fell behind and the road plunged into drowning space, pointed arrow straight at the mountains so vague in the distance.

At four o'clock the road dipped into a lava break running like a trough across the flats and came upon another roadhouse hidden beneath the wind, and presently the new relay hurried the coach on through late afternoon's changing light toward a visual breakthrough point. The distant mountains took on solid shape and moved gradually forward until at seven o'clock the desert broke upon timbered foot slopes as sea breaks against headlands. The road made its first turn in fifty miles and disappeared into tiers of pine which rose into an enormous yonder ruggedness. A creek came down from the heights, immediately to lose itself in the desert's sucking earth; beside the creek, backed against the timber, sat O'Fallen's roadhouse.

"Ten minutes behind," said Rheinmiller. "That Bessie mare soldiered on me."

Rawson dropped from the coach to stamp life into his dull legs. The passengers descended owl-sober and jaded, von Stern turning to offer Evelyn his hand. She came lightly to the ground and looked at once to the hills, her face quickened by the view of those hulking heights. "Mountain change—I smell it." The house light briskly flickered in her eyes. *Light, any kind of lights, sought her out*, Rawson thought.

They entered the single room of the roadhouse and sat down to supper. Rawson spoke to Evelyn. "That's a pretty dress."

"It's time you noticed."

"Not my business to notice," he said and lighted a cigar.

"It's every man's business to notice."

"Some man's, but not every man's."

Von Stern sat silent with his coffee, watching these two with his withdrawn manner. The room's warmth, the ride, or the heaviness of his thoughts seemed to have tired him. Now and then his glance settled on Rawson. Evelyn touched his arm. "Hugh's making a speech to me."

"Hope you understand it. I don't."

"I understand it," she said.

Barney Rheinmiller stacked coffee cup and saucer on his plate, laid knife and fork over them, and left the table. "Anybody coming with me, better come," he said.

Evelyn rose and walked from the room, followed by von Stern, Rawson, and the drummer; the rancher and the stranger remained, both to strike out by horseback in early morning along a forty-mile trail into another part of the mountains. Night laid its full back weight upon the land, the stars were very bright, the mountains lay blackly lumped before them. O'Fallen waited beside the new horses, reins in his hand. Von Stern climbed over the wheel to sit beside Rheinmiller. The drummer walked straight by the girl and into the coach. Rawson spoke to O'Fallen.

"Piutes moving around?"

"Too early. They ain't got the winter crimp out of their backs. Saw one last week. Took a shot. Long shot. Missed."

Rawson cast his cigar aside and followed Evelyn into the coach. "I'll sleep a little."

"Sit here. I've got the robe."

He settled beside her on the back seat and braced his long legs under the jump, the sudden forward rush of the horses throwing him against the cushions. O'Fallen shouted his farewell, the house lights died, and the coach swung into the climbing mountain road, into the profound darkness and the biting chill of the mountain's timber.

In the small hours Evelyn's restless turning woke him, and he doubled his half of the robe back over her shoulders, and heard her small protest. He said, "No point in both of us being half-miserable." He hunched his shoulders against the drafts and watched morning's first light dilute the dense night. At Roughneck Creek the trees began to stand out individually; by five o'clock, crawling up the hairpin turns of Jumpoff Joe, day washed the world with a sunless, pearled clarity. The coach, reaching the summit of this grade, entered the narrow turns of Echo Canyon and at seven rolled into the meadow at Head of the Mountain and stopped before Lasswell's roadhouse.

It was the end of Rheinmiller's run and he, chilled red face showing above a bulky Army overcoat, threw the reins down to the waiting Lasswell and came off the coach like a cranky bear backing out of a tree. Bart Lennon, silver hair and silver mustache against a peaceful brown face, stepped through Lasswell's doorway as soon as he saw Rawson. He took Rawson's hand and gave it a vigorous pumping. "Didn't expect you for a week. You well?"

"Fine as a frog in a puddle." Rawson turned and supported Evelyn as she descended. The shaking of the ride and the stiffness of her body unsettled her and for a moment she held to Rawson, laughing at herself. "Hello, Bart."

"You soak up some coffee and some heat," said Bart Lennon.

"Twenty minutes for breakfast," said Rawson. "From here on you're behind a highball driver."

"You or me?" said Bart.

"You think I came back to take in laundry?"

Von Stern and the drummer stood by in short-tempered silence. Bart Lennon's faded blue eyes surveyed Rawson and his mouth made its old man's kind smile. "All strutted up to crow, ain't you? And ready to peck. Get your breakfast."

Away from Lasswell's the mountain corridor ran, its spring grasses glazed by a dew which glittered in fractured brilliance under the sun. Cupped in by pine slopes all around and touched by the shadow of summits rising still higher against the blue, it lay as one of a hundred such miniature natural parks scattered through these tangled hills. The road, straining on for Ophir, made a yellow track across the meadow, now and then passing through small clumps of scattered timber. The last chill left the air and the smell of the mountains—pine resin and fragrant forest carpet and damp coverts in which ten thousand years of forest mold sunlessly lay—came strongly around Rawson, well-remembered, greatly missed, and now savored in silent relish. Rawson drove with his body swinging to the coach; he called briskly to the near wheeler slyly soldiering in the harness. "Any changes, Bart?"

"Marsh is pretty wet. This comin' back your idea, or was it Mulvey that pushed you to it?"

"Mine."

Lennon bent down to relight his pipe under the flap of his coat. He settled on the seat, crossed his legs and laced his hands behind his neck. "Never caught any sight of that fellow before he shot?"

"No."

"Might have been one man or a dozen back there in the trees that day. Poor show, Hughie. What's your intention?"

"Go after him."

"You don't know who you're lookin' for."

"I'll play for the break."

"Sittin' up here three times a week, cold meat? That makes no sense whatever. He was twenty-five feet away when he fired. I hunted up the tree and measured. So it was too close to be an accident, and I can't see why he didn't hit you straight. Who hates you that much?"

"I think it was a cripple shot intended to scare me off the run. That makes it more than one man. I think it's a gang, planning on the future."

"That's what I believe, too. We don't carry dust more than once every four trips. How could a man out in Camas Marsh know which trip was worth holding up unless he had somebody spotting for him in Ophir? That makes at least two—the spotter and the man who did the shootin'. We don't pack the box till the morning we go. So nobody knows till then. But when we lift the box to the seat it'd be easy for anybody to tell if it was heavy or light. That's five minutes before we pull out. The spotter, using a ridge trail, could short-cut us to the marsh by half an hour."

"This gold business is pretty fat. It's not a small man's game—it's a smart man's game, and he's got help. I want to tell you what I think, Bart, later in camp."

"I might be in it, and then you'd tip your hand to me."

"At sixty-five, what would you want with that much money? I had six weeks to separate the sheep from the goats. I separated you quick. I've got to trust somebody, or this is a pretty miserable world. I'll start with you."

"Better end right there. You like to believe

in your friends, but it won't do. It'll kill you."

"I limp a little and maybe always will. A limping man's not the same as a kid with nothing on his mind."

"Hughie," said Bart Lennon, "are you comin' back this time just to prove to Ophir you've got nerve? That's a hell of a reason."

"I expect to be a rancher in this valley the rest of my life. If I quit this job I'd have a reputation for backing down and every neighbor in the hills would try to take a fall out of me for the next fifty years. It won't do."

The valley grew narrower as it ran eastward, heavy hills rising to left and right, and during early afternoon the road approached a dark barrier of trees directly forward. At this barrier's edge, and hugging the road, sat Fay Miller's, its newly peeled logs shining in the sun; out upon the grassy open land some cattle grazed. Since it was not a stage stop, Rawson ran by the cabin. Behind the cabin, a young man turned a saddled horse, placing his back to the coach.

"Who's that new one?"

"Drifted in a month back unknown to me. Don't see Fay's horse, so he's in the hills. Hughie, this place don't signify."

"Not for a ranch," said Rawson. "It's too close to the marsh. Be a good place though for a man that wanted to duck in and out of cover in a hurry."

A hundred yards beyond Miller's dust

ceased to rise from the wheels and the coach passed into the timber, into a strong-flavored shade, into another world. This was the low end of the valley; it was a sump into which the creeks of the surrounding hills fell and sluggishly played in search of an outlet long since clogged by beaver dams. The result was a quivering black-soiled bog four miles wide, covered with timber alive and dead and dying, and so interlaced with fallen snags and faint-traced animal trails that it seemed like a piece of prehistoric jungle surviving in the heart of the hills. The road turned constantly in search of solid ground, roughened by the corduroy logs originally on the surface but now sucked below a mud which flew loosely away from the feet of the horses.

Half through the marsh the road swung about the perfect circle of a lagoon in which skinny-necked birds stood on their stilted legs; farther on a piece of semidry ground appeared and a trail led away from the road to some unknown place in the swamp.

"This is the place," said Lennon.

"He was behind that tree with the crooked foot," said Rawson.

It was a two-hour passage through the place. At five o'clock they broke clear of it and came upon Pennoyer's roadhouse in its meadow. A considerable group of men stood in the yard, drawing Lennon's interest.

"Something up."

Rawson lifted the horses into a last run and brought the coach to a spectacular stop before the antler-studded wall of Pennoyer's roadhouse, and before Pennoyer himself who waited here to catch the reins Rawson dropped to him. Slightly beyond the house half-a-dozen miners faced four cavalrymen and a tall lieutenant who had one hand draped over the shoulders of a small man.

Rawson said, "Hello," to Pennoyer and dropped to the ground. It was a casual greeting and neither man offered to shake hands. Rawson's voice caught the lieutenant's interest and he strode forward with a delighted wonder. "Hughie, I'll be damned." Laughing, he laid his two hands on Rawson's shoulders and shook them.

"Well," said Rawson, "you're wintered down." He gave this lieutenant, Adna Romillys Carrico, 3rd Cavalry, a short shove and grinned at him. "You're skinny from riding around interfering in other people's business."

Von Stern and Evelyn came from the coach and Evelyn watched the hearty show of affection between the men. Carrico was of much the same build as Rawson, slightly under six feet, long legs and chest, small hips, a fair skin and curled yellow hair which, though he was only thirty, showed a streaking on his temples. What set him apart from Rawson was an electric energy which warmed his face and glowed from his wonderfully blue eyes. His uniform was mud-splashed and a day's growth of whiskers darkened his jaws. Seeing Evelyn, he removed his forage cap and made a bow toward her. "I've missed you."

"That's nice," she said.

"Lieutenant," called a trooper.

Evelyn turned into the cabin. Carrico moved across to the group, Rawson and von Stern and Bart Lennon with him. The trooper spoke again. "What was your order, Lieutenant?"

Troopers and civilians made a loose ring around a dejected and bitter-eyed little man of about twenty-five. He had no hat, his clothes were crusted with mud, and a new scar crossed one side of his face. Rawson spoke to him. "What's up, Potter?"

Potter shrugged his shoulders without looking directly at Rawson. Carrico pointed to the group of prospectors. "These fellows chased him down from Muddy Bar. He was just ready to join his ancestors when I came along. They think he's been fooling with their sluice boxes."

One of the prospectors said, "You just go home, Carrico. Your business is to chase Piutes."

"You can't hang anybody around here on suspicion," said Carrico patiently. "Sergeant, take Potter to Camp Wilson and lock him up. When this blows over we'll see he gets a trial."

"I know your style," said the miner. "You'll

turn him loose. It won't do any good. We'll catch him again." He looked around and nodded toward von Stern. "What would you do, George?"

Von Stern had been watching Potter with a gloomy disinterest. He stared at the miner a moment, half-surprised by the question, and again studied Potter, as though the latter were scarcely more than a carcass of beef. He shrugged. "Hell," he said, "hang him and be done with it."

The answer was clearly a shock to Potter who stiffened his body and gave von Stern a piercingly direct stare; strong emotion placed a moment of resolution on his otherwise weak face and he drew a deep breath. But, on the edge of speech, the fire went out of him and he dropped his chin to resume his slack indifference.

"And what would you do, Hugh?" said the miner, pressing his advantage.

Rawson shook his head. "Carrico's right."

"Sure, sure," said the miner in discontent. "You'd stick with him. But of all men, you ought to know a damned sight better." He turned, looking beyond the group to a man leaning against the trunk of a near-by pine in the yard. "Fay, what you think?"

With the shadows of the tree upon him, Miller had rested quietly back, unobserved by the people of the coach, and when Rawson's glance turned to him he met it with a direct-

ness which was both guarded and alert and
in a degree insolent. He had one hand, the left
hand with its crooked fourth finger, jammed
into a trouser pocket; his rough and tumble
shoulders rested against the tree and he
seemed to be only a spectator laughing at the
audience. Yellow hair, far yellower than Carrico's, lay like hanks of yarn beneath his hat.
He gave Rawson no more recognition than
Rawson gave him, but he studied von Stern
for a moment before he shook his head at the
miner.

"None of my business," he said.

"Sergeant," said Carrico, "take Potter to
camp. That's the end of the nonsense."

"The hell it is," said the miner. "You can
lock him up, but wait till he gets out. Come
on."

The prospectors, soon on their horses, ran
out of the yard and the troopers swung up
and waited for Potter to pull himself from
his listless manner. He said, "Thanks, Lieutenant," and nodded to Rawson. Then the
venom of outrage gave to this weak man his
moment of incalculable wickedness and he
stared at von Stern out of flat-lighted eyes
and turned to his horse. Never once did he
look toward Fay Miller.

Rawson said, "We're wasting time," and
walked to the washbasin on its table at the
corner of the cabin. The rest of the party went
inside, Miller joining them. When Rawson

had scrubbed up he stood a moment, listening to Pennoyer as the latter cursed the new relay horses into harness. Westward he saw clouds gathering for a violent spring storm; the day's fine light had begun to catch late afternoon's amber shades. Then he went in to the supper table; he spoke to Mrs. Pennoyer who moved about with the food.

The trip had worn on von Stern's nerves and his voice was rough. "Someday that marsh road's going to drop right out from under the coach."

"Beavers keep backing it up with their dams," said Lennon. "One good ditch or a few sticks of dynamite would drain it quick."

For some reason the comment drew Fay Miller's interest. He raised his head from the plate. "What for? Nothing wrong with the road. Why change it?"

"To make it safe," said Lennon.

"Safe now."

"We ain't talkin' about the same thing," said Lennon quietly.

"I'm talking about the road," said Miller. He sat back on his chair, right hand lying in view, the crippled left hand out of sight. Discontented vitality gave his smile its edge of malice and made his voice unpleasantly blunt; he seemed to be inwardly laughing at them and still he was like a man waiting for something to be said that he might challenge.

"It's not a ditch the marsh needs," said Rawson.

"Now there's a good driver talkin'," said Fay Miller. "And proud of it, too."

Von Stern sent a quick cloudy glance toward Miller and withdrew it. Lennon watched the man with steady mildness while Carrico, a seemingly detached spectator, was mildly amused.

"What it needs," said Rawson, "is a couple of bullets well used."

"In that stuff," said Fay Miller, you'll need both hands for swimmin', but maybe you're one of these fellows that can swim and shoot at the same time."

Rawson patted the salt cellar and seasoned his meat. "No, I'll do what the fellow did who shot me—I'll stand on solid ground behind a tree. But I won't be as nervous as he was. I won't miss at twenty-five feet." He ate on, paying no attention to the others.

"Maybe," said Miller, his voice continuing with its small edge of sarcasm, "the man got somethin' in his eye when he fired, or maybe he was aimin' where he meant to aim. At twenty-five feet I'd say he ought to give up shootin' if he really missed."

"One thing or the other," said Rawson, "it was his mistake."

"Think it worries him a lot?" said Miller.

"So long as there's trees for him to hide behind, maybe he doesn't." Rawson finished his

30

coffee and reached for a cigar. He took his time lighting it; his face showed the fine enjoyment of the smoke's fragrance. "I've speculated on that fellow. Don't understand him. He likes to cripple his game before he kills it, never willing to let the game get a look at him. Matter of nerve, I guess. I don't think he's got any. I think he's yellow from his socks to his hat." He hunted for the words he wanted with evident enjoyment. He hadn't looked toward Miller, the girl noticed, but now he settled his glance on the man, an unruffled and mild glance. "I'm hunting for him and he shouldn't be hard to find. Not many men of that kind around here. I don't think he thought this up by himself. I think his britches are bought and paid for by somebody else, and there's another man I want to see. That's what I came back for. I propose to find both men."

The passengers came out and stepped into the coach. Carrico stopped in the yard, Fay Miller watched from the doorway, and Lennon crawled over the wheel to his side of the high seat. Carrico said, "I'll be in Ophir tomorrow—I want to talk to you."

Evelyn called from the coach. "You and Hugh and George are eating with me tomorrow night. Get your drinks before you come."

Rawson kicked the brake and shouted the team forward.

Lennon said, "You do surprise me, Hughie.

31

That was your war whoop, no mistake. You lighted a bonfire."

"Two bonfires," said Rawson.

"It ain't that certain."

"No, and I'd like to be wrong about some of it. We'll see, Bart. We'll soon see."

They had left Pennoyer's at five-thirty. Two hours later, from the ridge summit, another valley opened below them, running into a gulch whose two walls rose high against the shadowed sky. Along the gulch the first evening lights of Ophir were twinkling and beyond Ophir the heavy hills slowly darkened.

Lennon mildly summed it up. "There must be two hundred thousand in dust stacked up in the saloon safe and in Easterline's safe. This spring the miners will take out an easy quarter million more. All of it's got to go to Klickitat in this coach. That's the honey drawin' the bears. It's the stacked up two hundred thousand we got to worry about. It's too big a jaw now and we got to move inside thirty days before it gets any bigger. There's your chore, Hughie, everybody knows it and there ain't a hell of a lot of people bettin' you can do it."

They left the ridge and rushed over the basin into the jaws of two high ridges; and at eight-thirty that night, thirty-seven hours from Klickitat, Rawson ran down Ophir's single street and drew in before the crowd which always waited for a coach arrival around George von Stern's saloon. A voice called, "Hello, Hugh—back for the fun?" Then another voice said, "Throw down the mail sacks." He tossed the reins to a hostler below, climbed from the box and walked toward the cabin, ten doors distant, which was both his home and the express office.

Rawson rose at five and lighted a fire in the steel-cold room and, took his bucket and stepped into the frigid shock of an early mountain air slowly stained by the unraveling smoke of five hundred tin chimneys. He crossed the street, passed between two log houses—Easterline's Store and von Stern's Paradise Saloon—to the creek, caught his water, and returned to shave. Then he went over to the saloon for his beans, bread, and coffee. There was no restaurant in town, but von Stern's Chinaman could always furnish breakfast from the free-lunch leftovers of the preceding night.

Von Stern presently joined him; dark skin red-glossed from shaving, white shirt stiff with starch, his curled and heavy hair well brushed. He said in the idlest way, "I didn't get that play against Fay Miller. You know something, or just speculating?"

"Could be one thing or the other."

Von Stern shrugged his shoulders as if it were of no importance, but his next question jolted Rawson. "You took a walk with Evelyn in Klickitat. Did she say anything about me?"

"No," Rawson said. "Something on your mind, George?"

Von Stern studied him closely. "No, nothing."

There was this moment between them, a moment in which things were not as they ought to be. Rawson rose, irritated at von Stern for bringing up the girl's name. "You play your hand your own way."

"Always have," said von Stern in a completely neutral voice; the statement could fall any direction. Then he added, "See you at supper. Come in beforehand and we'll have a drink."

Rawson walked along the crooked street, with von Stern's question inflicting its nettle sting. Von Stern hadn't really meant it as a question, for the man was much too close-mouthed to open up his private affairs to anybody else; what it amounted to, actually, was a suggestion to Rawson to stay away from Evelyn. As soon as he understood it, Rawson grew very thoughtful. The long friendship was dying. It had begun to die the moment he had begun to suspect that George might be in the holdup business. He didn't wish to believe it and greatly hoped events would show him to be wrong; yet even if it turned out so, the original suspicion would have killed the friendship. Nobody could undo that change. George had sensed it; his reaction was to issue his warning.

He stepped into Easterline's Store; he shook hands with Ruel Easterline and ordered a few groceries and said, "I'll pick up the dust you've got in the safe, tonight or tomorrow," and waited while the storekeeper got his order together, vainly trying to summon up a decent interest in this colorless man. At thirty-five, Ruel Easterline might as well have been fifty or sixty for all the difference it made. Grave and neutral, with a visible anxiety to please people, he evoked no strong reaction of any sort from Rawson, who felt that it was difficult to pity Easterline for having an unfaithful wife. But neither was it possible for him to condemn Beth Easterline for wanting something her husband could not supply. It was one of those bad deals which happened to people.

Rawson walked to the side arch of Bailey Powell's blacksmith shop and stepped into the racket of Powell's hammer swinging down upon the anvil. Powell swung the ironwork back into the forge fire and came about to catch Rawson's hand with a fist as hard as the hoof on which he worked; his saddle brown eyes sent out a favorable beaming. "Good boy, Hugh," he said. "Limpin'?"

"Maybe it'll straighten out."

"Hope so." He lighted his pipe, and sat down on an upended tub, great arms slack over spraddled legs. "Back to drivin'?"

"Yes."

35

"Ah," said Powell, and gave his head half a shake and half a nod. It was impossible to know whether the gesture meant assent or regret for, with the beard so wholly covering him, Powell was a faceless giant made further dumb by a lack of ability with words.

Rawson strolled past the forge to the shop's rear doorway, it opening upon a gravel bar not much more than ten feet from the creek's high springtime stage. Across the creek a log barn sat on the narrow gravel strip, with a pole corral enclosing a dozen wild and runty horses which Veen Tilson, the Texas horse trader, sold to the miners after a casual breaking. Zigzag trails ran up the face of the mountain and disappeared into the thick hill timber. At this moment Tilson sat on a bench before his barn, warming himself in the first strong sunlight and seeming to study something higher along the gulch. Rawson presently spoke over his shoulder.

"Tilson still ride that calico horse with the marble eyes?"

"He does."

Rawson's attention moved to staggered pathways of the mountain's side. "Bailey," he said, "how often do you shoe that calico horse?"

"Maybe every month."

"Pretty often," said Rawson. "Means a lot of riding." He returned to the street and met Bart Lennon coming down from the upper part of camp. He made a motion at Bart and the two, turning, swung into the stiff-pitched wagon road which climbed the north wall of the gulch to a burying place on the summit flat. The ground at the bottom of Ophir gulch, containing gold, was too expensive for the dead. Halfway up, the cabins well below, the two squatted against the incline.

"Easterline's out of it," said Rawson. "He's not tough enough to be a crook. But Tilson won't lie straight in my head."

"He could be the fellow carryin' the news from here to somebody in the marsh."

"There's only two places on the road to worry about, the marsh—which is a perfect spot for a holdup—and in the timber between Head of the Mountain and the desert. We're going to try something, Bart. You take the stage out in the morning. Tonight I'll draw some of the dust from Easterline's safe, nobody else knowing, load it in a couple of saddlebags and make a roundabout run. I'll meet the coach at Head of the Mountain— in the canyon. Rheinmiller can take it from there."

Lennon shook his head. "That's just a little jag. Won't make a dent in the stuff stored up. I don't see any way to sneak it through. We've got to put it on the stage and make the run."

"It's just a fooler, Bart. I'll tell George what I'm doing. If the news leaks, we'll know how."

Bart looked squarely at Rawson. "Feel bad if he's in it?"

"I wouldn't like it, Bart." Rawson snapped a stunted grass stem and put it in a corner of his mouth. "He's been my friend for a long time."

At suppertime, Rawson crossed to the saloon, and found von Stern and Carrico waiting for him at the corner table. "You've delayed my drinking," said Carrico. "Where've you been?"

"Riding around."

Von Stern filled the glasses around and Carrico said, "How," and they downed the whiskey. Von Stern had shaved again, his face showing the ruddy glow of hot towels, fresh shirt straining against his coat. He said to Rawson, "Ride up the gulch?"

"Here and there," said Rawson.

Carrico smiled. "The information just pours out of him." He observed the settling of von Stern's expression, and his own manner grew thoughtful.

Veen Tilson shouldered himself from the crowd around the bar and walked to the table, drawing back a chair as if to join the others; at that moment von Stern's eyes struck him with a hooded irritation, the effect of it like a strong push, and Tilson checked himself. He was a small, wire-drawn man with a cowhand's sprung legs and a dry face deeply corroded by seams of rough living. He stood half-faced about, and his smile, reaching Rawson from this angle, was sly and over-friendly. "Glad to see you, boy. I was thinkin' —that bay of yours is old. You ought to let me trade you a better horse."

"No," said Rawson. This man was no friend of his, and he knew it, and yet used the familiar manner deliberately; he was a cheap scoundrel with no reputation and too much brass, and secretly contemptuous of those upon whom he imposed. Behind him, Rawson suddenly noticed, Fay Miller stood near the bar, watching this scene with his flushed and acidly amused countenance. If his guess were right, these three men were against him— Miller and Tilson and George. What brought them together under one roof? Veen Tilson, still smiling, walked around the table and clapped his hand briskly on Rawson's shoulder.

"Well, boy, you need a better horse."

Rawson turned to catch von Stern's expression, and found only a shrewdly dulled poker mask. *Might find out something here*, he thought, and said aloud to Tilson, "Take your damned hand off me."

The man's smile remained, growing tighter until the lips were fish-creased. *Maybe*, thought Rawson, *he wants to make a sucker out of men in front of the camp. There's some reason for this. His reason, or Miller's or George's.* He shifted his body and gave Tilson

a full-armed shove which sent the man backward and off his feet to the floor. Rawson
bent forward on the chair, hands propped
against his kneecaps for a quick jump. Tilson
rose from the floor, the skin of his face grey
and wrinkled; he passed a hand over his skull,
he looked quickly around—it might have
been toward Miller, or von Stern, or anybody.
In his eyes the furnace doors were wide open.
There, thought Rawson, *danced the devil*.

"I ought to stamp your guts out," said Tilson.

Rawson shoved himself from the chair,
watching Tilson's arm whip behind his coat
toward his trouser band; he came in quickly
to stop the knife he knew was there, he hit
Tilson flat-fisted on the face, he clubbed the
man's trapped arm downward, and caught
him and rushed him backward against the
saloon wall. He drew him away from the
wall and threw him into it with a full shove
of back and shoulders. The horse trader
dropped on his knees. He coughed and let his
head bob, but he said, "I'm goin' to kill you—"

Von Stern's voice leaped at him. "Shut up,
Tilson. You can't come in my place and pull
a ruckus."

Tilson came off the floor, breath rustling
through a wide-open mouth. He said, "All
right—all right," and brushed himself, and
touched his face, and looked at his finger tips.
He avoided Rawson's eyes and sent a quick,

strange glance at von Stern. *That's it*, thought Rawson, *there's his boss*. He said to Tilson, "Keep away from me. Next time you try to make me look foolish in front of a crowd, I'll break your neck." He passed into the crisp night, waiting there. Carrico and von Stern presently joined him and the three moved toward Evelyn Harvey's cabin.

Carrico said, "What was that all about?"

"Nothing."

"That was poor judgment," said von Stern. "You made an enemy. What for?"

Evelyn's door stood open and she came from the rear room. "Have you had your drinks?"

"Yes," said Carrico. He removed his hat and stared at her with open, admiring directness.

She turned to Rawson and von Stern. "Why are you solemn?"

Carrico said, "Hugh went out in the open market and bought himself a fight," and explained it to the girl. "George and I don't know why."

"I do," she said.

Von Stern said, "Why?"

"Because," she said, and touched Rawson's arm, the light dancing brightly in her eyes. She was again for him like crystal, all color and motion, and her presence squeezed sensation out of strange places into his nerves and this sensation ran fully through him. Evelyn said, "Sit down," and turned into the kitchen. The three men settled themselves, crowded between the table and the dress dummy and the shelves of bolt goods along the wall.

Early springtime darkness flowed into the canyon while they ate, and lanterns bobbed past the house. Somewhere in the camp's upper part of the music of a guitar and fiddle unevenly rose and fell. Von Stern looked at Carrico. "I guess we better let go on Hugh."

"Go ahead."

"Hugh," said von Stern, "you've got no show. You're out in the open—other fellow's in the brush. No sport in camp would lay three to one money on your lasting ninety days if you try to drive through to Klickitat with the dust. It's maybe a matter of pride for you to prove you can't be bluffed. Go ahead and get killed to prove it, and what good is that to you? It's a bad deal. I think it, Ad thinks it. All your friends do. So does Evelyn."

"I haven't said," she put in. "Anyhow, you're using the wrong argument on him."

"What's a better one?"

"None. He made up his mind in Portland."

"I wasn't aware of that," said von Stern, coolness in his tone.

Carrico tried his luck. "It takes a certain kind of man to survive this business, the kind who thinks all other men are dogs out to bite him. You're not that kind."

"That's closer," said Evelyn, "but it won't change him."

Von Stern pointed a stiff forefinger at Rawson. "You want to start a ranch in Deer Valley. You're working to build up a stake, but at two hundred a month it'll be forever. Quit driving and I'll stake you up to $2500. Pay it back when you make the grade."

Rawson shrugged his shoulders. "Nice to have friends. You can dig my grave when the time comes."

"I'll talk to him," said Evelyn. "You two go away."

Carrico turned and put his hand on von Stern's arm, drawing him to the door; before passing through he looked back, now entirely smiling. "The strategy is clever."

She burst into laughter. "Oh, Ad, you're half a sinner and half a saint."

"Which is better?" he asked, and pulled a silent von Stern into the night.

Rawson watched her manner swiftly swing. She showed restlessness and moved to the door and watched the street. Then she turned. "You think a lot of things about me. I wish you'd say some of them so I could put you right."

He rose and stacked his dishes and walked into the kitchen. "Come on."

"I'll do that later. I want to talk."

"Talk with your hands in water." Then he turned to her. "You worried about George

43

outside and me inside? Maybe I'd better go."

She came into the kitchen with a short-tempered expression. She put on her apron and filled the dishpan while he got a towel. She said, "You're dumb at the wrong times."

They finished the job in silence. He hung the towel back of the stove and got an armload of wood from the shed for the woodbox. He sat on the woodbox, full and comfortable and sleepy; contentment was a drug turning him wonderfully stupid. She had left on the coffeepot and now poured a cup for both of them.

"You'll be set like iron in your ways when you're an old man," she said. The night air, coming through the front door, chilled her and she rose and closed it and came back to the kitchen.

He said, "George will be here ten minutes after I'm gone—sore. That why you're doing this?"

She turned, her mouth honey-smooth with its amusement. Shock came again to him and he held her glance until the amusement withdrew from her and the aloofness vanished. He closed his eyes, the fire's warmth soaking into his bones until he weighed a thousand pounds. He had no thoughts at all, only the sensation of complete well-being.

She said, "A fine thing, sleeping in my woodbox. Go home to bed."

He rose and went to the door. "You and George having a little trouble?"

"Turn around and tell me what made you ask."

"He wanted to know if you'd said anything about him on our walk in Klickitat."

She was silent and in argument with herself; by the tightening of her features, he saw her go over some disagreeable jump. "That sounds as though he has rights, doesn't it?"

"George is no Carrico for light nonsense. He's jealous."

"Do you think he has any rights?"

"You want to know what I think?"

"I know what you think. I want you to say it."

"Well, hasn't he?" He turned away. She said nothing when he closed the door behind him.

She walked to the back room, poured herself another cup of coffee, and sat on the kitchen chair. She looked into the cup as a gypsy looks into a magic brew, her face turned peaceful. She thought of the friendship between Hugh, Carrico, and von Stern, and realized it was dying. Men were strange creatures to whom friendships meant much, and when friendship vanished they were saddened without saying so. She had known for many weeks that Hugh had looked at her with his private thoughts and yet, because he believed her to be von Stern's choice, he had stayed quiet. That was friendship. Yet she knew too that when these two men no longer trusted each other—and she saw that suspicion beginning—Hugh Rawson might still stay quiet; for he had other thoughts about her which put a barrier between. There was nothing she could do about it.

She heard the sudden solid fist on the door, three blunt raps identifying George. She sat still. She thought: *I ought to end this now. I ought to let him in and tell him.* She heard him speak. "Evelyn, I'd like to talk to you." *No,* she thought, *I'll wait.*

"I'm in bed, George."

There was no sound from him and she visualized him rankly angered in the darkness, half-disposed to quarrel; his temper, when roused, was like dull red iron sullenly shining. Presently she heard him turn away.

From the window of the store's living quarters, Beth Easterline watched Evelyn's place until she saw Carrico leave it with von Stern. She thought: *Damn you for wasting time in her place,* and haste got into her and she finished the supper dishwashing as fast as possible. She threw on her coat and stepped into the store. Easterline was at his account book, the yellow light not kind to his face. She said, "I've got to get out of here—I'm going for a walk."

"There's a drunk or two around. Be a little careful."

"I'll be careful," she said.

Directly beyond the store she turned into the rough road which led to the burial grounds at the top of the ridge. She walked so rapidly that she was out of breath when she reached the summit and saw the shadow of horse and man a short distance away. She went immediately to Carrico and stepped into his arms with a sighing delight at his roughness.

He untied a blanket behind the saddle and threw it to the ground, the two settling on it. He said, "This is miserable business."

"I don't mind. At least we have this much."

"Something's got to be done," he said. "The camp's going to start talking. I can't have you muddied up by that. I've been trying to think a way out of it—"

She said, "There's no way. Don't worry. It doesn't matter. I don't care if Ruel finds out —that's how far I've gone. When I see you, I'm happy. In between, I'm dead."

Her lips hunted over his face with her liveliness and found his mouth and pressed heavily against it. He pulled her nearer, and locked his arms about her. She shook, she made a queer sound in her chest, and was afterwards still. The grazing horse drifted away.

The moment Rawson stepped into his cabin the sensation of danger prickled through him. He stopped, one foot ahead of the other, and swung his head to orient the man he knew was there.

"It's all right," said a voice. "I'm in your back room."

"Who's that?"

"Potter."

He struck a match to the table lamp and saw the man's pack-rat face hooked around the casing of the kitchen door. He turned the lampwick down to a thin rind of light. "How'd you get out of Carrico's guardhouse?"

"He opened the door and told me to walk."

That would be Carrico's way, to balance this small human being against the crowd and to decide against the crowd. "You're not smart," said Rawson. "You're fair game for any man's gun."

"You did me a favor—and I can do you one. I need some grub."

Rawson found a linen sack and walked to the grub shelf. He dumped some flour into the sack and a two-pound chunk of bacon; he threw in his small sack of coffee, a bag of salt, and his can of baking powder. "That'll take you to Klickitat, and if you're smart you'll not stop till you get there."

Potter said, "You know why you got knocked off that coach?"

"You tell me."

"They figured there'd be no more shipments for awhile. That backs up a lot of dust here and when you load the express box, it'll be a big load. They want that—not a lot of little jags slippin' through their fingers trip after trip, but one big chunk of gold they can grab and run with."

"Who's they?"

The little man teetered one hand back and forth. "They're here in Ophir, and out on the road. I never was in with 'em, but I see a lot, riding around."

"You're guessing, Potter."

Potter shook his head. "If you see enough, you can guess pretty straight. They know it too. You think it's the miners I'm worried about? Not a bit. It's the other crowd that I'm duckin'!"

"Better start then."

Potter rose and slipped to the door. "Take the trail along the ridge and cut off toward the marsh. See what you find." He slid through the door and closed it quietly.

Rawson whipped out the light, and left the cabin, going directly to the stable. He saddled, moved fifty yards along the street, and stepped into the gap between Easterline's Store, went in, and came out again in fifteen minutes with two saddlebags filled with dust from Easterline's safe. There were no lights in Tilson's barn when he crossed the creek and moved up the trail, but at the summit corral he saw the shape of Tilson's calico. He passed into the thoroughly black trail.

Tilson, during that time, squatted halfway

up the east wall of the gulch, waiting to identify the walking shadow he had earlier noted climbing the cemetery road. Having this bird's-eye view, he saw a man come from Rawson's cabin, reach a horse, and angle up the hill. When he crossed the cemetery road he was within ten feet of Tilson who, flat on the ground, identified him.

He had no gun, or he would have shot Potter at that moment. He lay silent until Potter disappeared, then scrambled down the hill and walked briskly to the saloon. He stepped into the crowd and moved around until he caught von Stern's attention. Immediately afterward he left the saloon, circled to a rear door, and entered a small room back of the bar, this being von Stern's bedroom. Von Stern presently came in, closed the door quickly behind him.

"I don't like this, Veen."

"I saw Potter. I think he came out of Rawson's. He's gone now."

Von Stern's face settled. He shook his head. "He didn't know much but it won't do."

"Might know more than we think. He was always sneakin' around the trail, watchin' for an easy miner to pick. I think he's got it sized up. If he's scared he'll head for Klickitat—but he's told Rawson something."

"I'll think about it," said von Stern. "You stay out of it. What were you trying to do tonight?"

"Damn the man—he can't shove me."

"Stay out of that, too. Every time you move you tip your hand, or mine. Where's Fay?"

"He started back."

"All right," said von Stern, and watched the horse trader open the door, pinch himself through the crack, and disappear. That, he thought, was the trouble—the bad judgment of the men he had to work with in this proposition.

Riding through the hard-shadowed mountains, Rawson went on until he was certain he had passed the mouth of the side trail to Portuguese Camp, drew off the trail, and rolled into his saddle blanket. He was in motion again at first daylight, a chilled man on an irritable horse. The sun rose bright above the pine tops, but in this constant shade the deep chill remained. Below him, though he couldn't see it, the military post of Camp Wilson lay, a half-dozen cabins and a stockade housing Carrico's skeleton company of cavalry.

Half an hour more of riding brought him to another side trail swinging down the mountain and this, remembering Potter's advice, he took. Three miles onward the trail forked, right-hand prong aiming directly for the swamp now not far away, left-hand prong swinging west of the swamp—and probably coming out behind Fay Miller's cabin.

He followed the right fork down the final pitch of the mountain directly into the edge of the swamp and found himself facing what seemed an impassable area. The trail ended here; yet when he looked more closely he saw it twisting from one semisolid hummock to another, skirting fallen trees and disappearing into rank brush. A black and odorous water lay everywhere, edged by an ancient, dull-shining mud; the horse, lowering his head for a better sight of such footing, stood still until he spurred it.

Cautiously traveling, he made a quarter mile before the resistance of the horse stopped him. He was on a miniature island twenty feet wide, looking across a ten-foot strip of dead water to another such island; the trail went into the water and came out again, but when he looked into the water he saw no fording place. He dropped from the saddle, got a yard-long dead branch, and plunged it through the slack pool into the bottom mud; the pole went full length and touched no bottom.

He crossed the brushy hummock to its other side and at once saw he had misread the trail; it came this way, followed the causeway of an old beaver dam, touched another hummock, and, by one devious turning and another, reached the island he saw across the strip of water. The mistake jarred him and he circled the hummock to find his back trail. In any direction, the view was the same—snags and thicket and live trees dying and these small steppingstone bits of solid earth surrounded by black-glittering water. He thought he sighted the way by which he had come and went immediately to his horse and turned about.

He lost himself twice again before finally reaching firm ground at the edge of the hills, and came out a good hundred yards from his entry point, quietly sweating. Nothing but experience would do in that place and, when the shadows began to settle on the marsh, not even experience would be much of a comfort. Yet whoever had shot him had come from the marsh, had used it for a shelter.

He returned to the trail on the crest of the ridge and followed this until, during the afternoon, it carried him gradually downward into Deer Valley behind Lasswell's place. He let the horse graze and settled himself to catnap through the mild day; toward suppertime he saw the stage break into view on the valley floor, and he rode a wide circle around Lasswell's to the stony gap which ran through Head of the Mountain and waited there.

He transferred the saddlebags to the stage when Barney came through an hour later, and turned back to Lasswell's for his supper. Bart Lennon, finished with his run, had already eaten and sat peacefully in the yard with his pipe, enjoying the soft-falling twilight; and after his meal, Rawson joined him for a smoke, giving his horse time for a bag of oats. As soon as that was done, Rawson turned homeward on the road.

Fay Miller's cabin was dark when he passed it. Within the marsh he was closed about by silence which was not silence—the surreptitious wake of things moving without echo, of a yeasty stirring beneath the mud, of nostrils flared to catch his odor as he passed, of living things turned to moment's stone when he rode near. The tension of the place worked on him so that the Pennoyer meadow, when he came upon it, was a relief. It was midnight, but a light burned in the cabin and a pair of horses stood at the door. He rode to the leanto, unsaddled, and walked back; when he entered he saw Pennoyer rising from a chair with a quick expression of surprise—of unusual surprise. Fay Miller and the stranger who stayed with Miller sat at the table, drinking coffee.

Pennoyer said, "I'll get some more coffee," and turned to the kitchen. *Caught him off guard,* Rawson thought. Was it surprise or something else? He moved to the fire and put his back to it. The stranger with Miller was a kid with a bony face, big eyes, and a bad look about him, and his clothes were dirtier than anybody's clothes ought to be.

Mrs. Pennoyer brought in the coffee to the kitchen. Rawson thought, *Pennoyer doesn't want to show up in this, whatever it is.* Fay Miller was idle, closely thinking, and rank vitality simmered in him and put its sullen shning in his eyes. "Why don't you stay in your own country?" he asked.

"When did we start settin' up different countries?"

"That swamp," said Miller, "is part of my ranch. Keep out of it."

"When did you file on it at the land office?" asked Rawson. He drank his coffee, watching Miller over the cup's rim.

The younger man, rising, began to circle the table toward the fire. Rawson spoke gently to him. "Don't get behind my back."

The younger man stopped; he turned his head toward Miller. Miller nodded at him. "Don't let anybody give you orders."

"I think that's bad advice," said Rawson.

"Turk," said Miller, "go around him if you want."

The younger man remained indecisive in his tracks, half-turned and half-strained by the position.

Miller said, "You bluff that easy?"

"Maybe he's smart enough not to carry another man's bucket," said Rawson. He rose, made half a swing, and stepped to the fire; he laid his back to it, keeping both men before him, and he began to think about Pennoyer somewhere around the cabin, or maybe outside looking through a window. He had to figure three to one if anything blew up.

Miller said, "You threw something at me the other day at the table. I didn't care much about it. Made me look funny in front of people. What was on your mind?"

"When somebody crowds me," said Rawson, "I crowd back."

Miller rose and came around the table. He stood three paces from Rawson with impulse and caution chasing each other across his face. He was close to a showdown. His wild temper carried him toward it, his coolness held him back. He threw a glance toward Turk who, after a moment's hesitation, walked around the table and paused near the kitchen door; this placed him at a more extreme angle of Rawson's vision, and Rawson called him.

"Don't stand there, Turk, unless you mean to start something."

"I'm just walkin' around," said Turk.

"Walk toward the front door," said Rawson, "where I can see you better."

"Do as you please, Turk," said Miller.

Rawson lifted his voice. "Mrs. Pennoyer, I think you'd better get out of the kitchen. You're in my line of fire."

Turk said, "Never mind," and walked over and stopped by the front door, behind Miller.

"What you made of—mush?" said Miller. Anger pushed him beyond his restraint. "Let's mix it right here. Drop your gun and I'll drop mine."

"I'll keep mine."

"I can take a fall out of you any day in the week," said Miller.

"Don't think you can. Want to try?"

"Just fists?"

"So long as that's your limit," said Rawson promptly. "If I see anything funny I won't stop to argue. Turk, stay where you are."

"I ain't moved," said Turk.

Miller stepped in, his hands idle; he stopped within reach of Rawson, firelight yellowing his eyes. What Rawson watched for was the signal of coming motion around Miller's mouth—the instant of lip pressure by which men betrayed themselves—and when he saw it he turned his body and knocked down Miller's left hand as it came in. He struck Miller in the stomach directly below the center joining of the ribs. It hurt Miller enough to stop him a moment and Rawson threw a punch into the man's face, and side-stepped and tried a far-swinging wallop into Miller's stomach. Miller's fist came out of a blind spot and seemed to blow off the top of his head. He threw up his arms and was badly beaten around the ribs before he got his guard down; he jumped back, Miller furiously rushing him, and he whirled aside and threw his shoulder at Miller as the latter went by. He was too slow to catch the man; he turned and saw Miller pull himself around. He jumped Miller, he slugged him in the belly and drove him against a chair which, catching Miller at the back of the legs, threw him. He landed on a shoulder, rolled catlike, and came up. He stood a moment, both arms feinting. He said, "I'm going to put you back in the hospital for another month." He dropped his head, rushing. Rawson knocked his arms down and took the full impact of the lower head on his chin. He gave ground, he hooked Miller in the face and got the man's head raised. Miller's beating blows knocked him left and right and swayed him. He rammed his skull into the man's nose and mouth, and jumped aside. Miller's quick feet danced around and he rushed, reaching and missing and crowding in. Rawson whirled, flung an arm about Miller's neck, and gave a sharp, turning, downward heave. He got behind Miller and locked his grip and stepped backward, dragging Miller off balance. The man's falling weight came upon his own neck and he began to kick out with his feet, striking nothing. His backward arm swings went by Rawson. Rawson held him thus suspended and watched him grow a deeper red. Then he dropped him and circled to keep Turk in his view.

Miller stood up, his eyes strained out and his mouth opened to a suckling circle; he bent over with a moment's agony of wanting wind, and thus left himself wide-open. Rawson ignored the target, for suddenly he had enough of it. His bad leg seemed a column of flame from ankle to hip. "That will be enough, Fay."

Miller was a mean bull, stunned for the

moment but still dangerous, his face the face of a man looking into some deep place. But then the insolence and the changeable mockery came quickly back. He turned and walked to the door and paused a moment to stare at the younger man. He spoke with a heavy sarcasm. "If you're not afraid of the dark, Turk, we'll ride home." He opened the door and stepped into the night. Turk, following, shut the door behind him.

That, thought Rawson, *is his second try at scaring me off the run.* He was as certain as he would ever be that Miller had taken the shot at him. It explained this business completely. From the corner of his eye he saw Pennoyer in the kitchen doorway.

Pennoyer said, "You stayin' here tonight?"

"Yes."

Pennoyer pointed to the corner room. "Use that," he said, and returned to the kitchen.

George von Stern, the following morning, left Ophir before daybreak, climbing the hill west of camp; steadily traveling through the rain, he reached the burn and at the next turnoff to the left he passed into a rough and heavily timbered gulch. A mile of this brought him to a mass of cabin-sized rocks tumbled into the gulch from the ridge parapets above and though the trail skirted these and followed the gulch to its head, he swung left again to follow the track of the slide until it struck the base of the ridge.

In some long-gone time these thousands of tons of rock, soil, and pine had tumbled down to lodge one upon another, now overgrown with another generation of timber. A vague pathway carried him directly toward an obvious dead end at the barrier of the slide; then, sharply swinging, it went around one of the rocks, passed through a stony aperture and stopped in a natural room created by the slide. It was large enough not only for von Stern and his horse but also for Fay Miller—who waited there—his horse, and a small fire Miller had built. The smoke curled upward, was caught by a current of wind and sucked deeper into the rock pile.

Miller said, "I been waiting two hours— damn dismal place."

"What happened to your face?"

"Had a fight with Rawson last night. What was he doing at Pennoyer's? It's up to Tilson to keep track of him."

Von Stern settled on his heels and laid his palms over the fire. "This dust business will break soon. He's got to get it out to Klickitat. If he tries to scatter a little bit on each trip he won't be able to cut the backlog down. He'll do what I'd do—load it on one run and try to make the drive through with four or five men riding guard in the coach."

"It's going to be lively," said Fay Miller.

"I expect you to figure the thing in such a way that there can't be any fight."

"Now, George, use your head. Of course there'll be a fight." He pointed a finger straight upon von Stern. "How much you think there'll be on that load?"

"About two hundred thousand. I don't want trouble, Fay."

"You're mixed up, George. You expect me to shoot around a man, but not hit him at a time like that when hell's apt to be comin' down the hill on a greased skid? Not possible."

Von Stern's muddy brown eyes rose on Miller. "That nervous finger of yours did it. The shooting wasn't necessary. Rawson's a well-liked man around camp, and all the sympathy's on his side. The upshot of it is the camp's wondering what goes on. You already started one piece of business you've got to finish in a hurry. Potter's loose. Carrico let him out of the guardhouse, and night before last Tilson saw him come from Rawson's cabin."

"He don't know much," said Miller. He grew thoughtful; he shook his head. "But the little weasel's probably picked up something by watching the trails."

"You take care of that," said von Stern. "And do it fast."

The hard rattling of rain on the cabin roof made the stove's warmth particularly cozy and comfortable. Evelyn had a pillow on the floor and knelt before Mrs. Easterline with her tape, measuring the woman for a dress. Mrs.

Easterline stood patiently. "What day's this?" she asked.

"Friday," said Evelyn and looked up to see the give-away expression around the mouth.

The fitting ended, Evelyn made a pot of tea and the two sat in the front room for idle chat. "I envy your skin," said Mrs. Easterline. "Mine's rough. It's the weather. I dread to think what I shall be like at forty."

"That's a long way off."

"Too close. Oh, well, it's of no account. Everything's accident anyhow, and even the good accidents come too late." Her eyes fell toward her cup. "Is there any talk around camp about me?"

Evelyn said, "Why don't you leave Ophir?"

"My husband makes a living here."

"Then go alone. You're certainly miserable in this place."

"I'd be more miserable away."

"Couldn't you and Ad do something about all this?"

"He does what the Army tells him. I couldn't ask him to resign. It's his profession. I couldn't divorce Easterline. That would be against Ad's record if he married me and I'd not be socially accepted in the Army."

"It sounds as though you've not asked Ad to do anything. Perhaps he would."

Beth Easterline shrugged her shoulders and met Evelyn's gaze with a matter-of-fact directness. She considered a moment and said,

"We'll just go on till something happens. He'll be transferred—that's the normal thing. Or he'll grow tired, or perhaps I will." Her smile came swiftly and sharply through her dramatic soberness. "I'll tell you something in confidence. I have no intentions of divorcing or leaving Easterline." Suddenly she laughed at Evelyn and left the cabin.

Evelyn washed the teacups and returned to the front room to continue work. But the desire had left her, the room was stuffy, and Beth Easterline's talk disturbed her. She wrapped a shawl around her head, covered herself with a heavy coat, and stepped into the rough afternoon to work off the accumulated pressure of thinking. A heavy stove smoke rolled from the chimney of Rawson's cabin. She had noticed him enter town an hour earlier and go by her door, clothes muddy and in need of a shave. Something of interest had kept him out in the hills for two days and she hoped he meant to stop in after he had taken care of himself and speak of it. But that she oughtn't to expect. He was in a hard game and couldn't say very much to anybody. She thought to herself: *Speak or not, just come.* Suddenly, two days was a long time to be away from a person one needed.

Two men with a loaded packhorse behind them rode up to the blacksmith shop; and men began to come up from various parts of the camp until there was half a crowd around the place. It was then at the beginning of the day's first greying; the wind had risen and the rain fell harder. Evelyn, still restless, walked on back to her cabin. She stuffed the stove with wood and lighted a lamp. Then, scarcely hungry, she brewed a pot of coffee, found a strip of cooked bacon from breakfast, and ate this with a bit of bread and a dish of boiled apricots. She found herself listening for someone at the door; but when somebody's knuckles *did* rap—the hard three raps of George von Stern's hand—a wave of shock went disagreeably through her. She drew a breath, said, "Come in," and watched him walk through the door.

He closed it and stepped toward her, the claylike gravity quite pronounced on his face. She knew the sign of temper; he had made up his mind on some subject and meant to bring it into the open. She motioned toward the room's other chair. He shook his head. "No, Evelyn. I want this settled. I've put in too many years at the poker table not to know change when I see it. I want to know what's changed with us."

She said, "Who was in the blacksmith shop —who'd they bring in?"

"Just another dead man. A little bum. Potter. Somebody shot him—over in Mulehide Gulch."

"The one Ad Carrico took away from the

miners?" She remembered the scene. "That's sad."

"What's sad about a man like that? For all the good he's done, or for the use in him, he might as well not have been born."

"You've not got much sympathy, George. I'd think you would have, seeing so much sadness in your saloon."

He still watched her, the somber shrewdness hanging on. "Where's the change, Evelyn?"

The insistence pressed upon her until she felt herself cornered. Her heart quickened. She had to push the words quickly out. "Don't come here any more."

"Why? Is it Hugh?"

"Nothing's been said about that."

"But is it?"

"George, don't embarrass me by speaking of it to him."

"You know he's got his doubts, don't you?"

She said, "Yes," then added, "but how do you know? Have you two talked about me?"

He shook his head. "Not necessary. I know what's in his head."

A moment of hope made its lively break over her face.

"George, do you think you could say something to him to make that straight?"

"From me?" he said. "Why should I do it? Would he believe me if I did?"

She made a little gesture. "No, it wouldn't do. Never mind."

He plunged both fists into his pockets and stirred heavily around the room and stopped in the corner behind her. "Evelyn," he said, "you're not a woman to spend your time in a shanty. You were made for beautiful clothes, a fine house, and all the trinkets. It's all over you. I can do that—Rawson never will."

"Those are not the things I want most."

"They were once," he said. "In the beginning you were fond of me."

"No, never quite. I was attracted. I thought about it—I've thought about you until quite recently, but never the way you wished."

"Why—why?"

"Nobody can explain why that happens."

He stared at her and she thought she saw the slow dark fire in this man brighten to a hotter emotion. She had suspected he could be dangerous and now she was sure of it. He hadn't grace enough or tolerance enough to be forgiving; he had so little of the humane qualities. Nodding, he turned through the door.

He stood outside the door a moment and then returned to his saloon. He saw Rawson at the bar and joined him. He motioned to the barkeep, got bottle and glasses, and silently poured two drinks. He made a short dip of the glass at Rawson, drank and pushed the bottle aside.

"Never noticed you drink at this time of day," said Rawson.

"Always comes a time when a man gets damned good and tired of his old habits." He laid his arms on the bar, resting the weight of his upper body on them. He nodded toward the safe. "That thing's getting full. New stuff's coming in. You want to put some of it in your safe?"

"I'll work it down, trip by trip."

"Better start. I don't like to keep that much dust around."

"Already started," said Rawson. "I took ten thousand from Easterline the other night and carried it horseback to Head of the Mountain. Rheinmiller carried it through from there."

"Don't do that. If it's found out, you'll never ride anywhere without the chance of being knocked over." He turned off to the small room in the corner, shut the door, and began a steady tramping back and forth, cigar smoldering between his teeth.

After von Stern's departure, there was no more work left in Evelyn. She sat a long while in the chair, reviewing the talk and made unhappy by the inconsistency she must have shown George. The scene had left her tired; yet the restlessness held on, and a feeling of being adrift grew strong. She rose to make herself coffee, and stood in the back room to drink it. But that didn't help and she got into her coat and left the cabin. She hadn't walked far in the rain, though, when she met Rawson, who had just left the saloon. "Not at night, Evelyn—it's not quite that safe," he said.

He took her arm and walked her back to her cabin. She opened the door, moved into it, and swung about. She wanted to talk to him, she wanted the talk to go on and on until it came out that she had broken with von Stern, but this was a more difficult thing than it had been and she stood irritably helpless, yet smiling and wishing to please him. "Where've you been?"

"Ramming around the hills."

She said, "I've got to see Mrs. Jeffroy someday at Portuguese Camp."

"If it's anything you want to take her, I'll do the chore for you in the morning. I'm going in that direction."

"No, I just promised to go see her. Is the trail all right?"

"Good enough. I don't know that you ought to go alone."

"Then let me ride with you."

"I won't be back until late."

"I'll come back alone—or wait."

His expression told her he was thinking of von Stern. She waited, strongly hoping he'd mention it; then she could tell him. Instead he nodded and said, "It will be early. Five in the morning."

"Come here first and I'll feed you."

"All right," he said. He remained a little

longer, not anxious to go and perhaps wishing to come in. But now she had to be careful with him and she said, "Good night, Hugh," and closed the door. She was unaccountably happy and looked at Mrs. Easterline's dress with the first energy of the day within her. "Now, you," she said, and sat down before it and began to work.

Rawson went into his cabin, walked directly out of it again by way of the shed door, and stepped along the back side of several cabins until he found a dark patch in the street, there crossing to Easterline's Store. He entered the rear way and stood a moment in the kitchen with Beth Easterline while the storekeeper filled a pair of saddlebags with dust from the safe.

Mrs. Easterline said, "Could I make you some coffee?"

"I've had a drink of pretty decent liquor—straight from von Stern's private bottle—and I want to keep the taste of it."

Easterline returned with the heavy saddlebags, and Rawson dropped back into the darkness, retracing his route to his own cabin. Bart Lennon was in the front room waiting for him. He watched Rawson toss the saddlebags into the safe and spin the dial on the door.

"I told von Stern tonight what I was doing," said Rawson.

"About this load?"

"No, about the last load. But if he's got a spotter he'll know about this one."

"Hell's fire," said Lennon. "You've asked for trouble. If they bushwhack you out in the timber, what good's it going to do you to discover von Stern's a crook? You'll be dead."

"No I won't, Bart. Decided not to die."

Bart Lennon was not satisfied by the answer and sat with his glumness showing. "Well, where you going to meet the stage tomorrow? Head of the Mountain again?"

"Not that far. I'll be in the second stand of timber you pass through beyond Miller's. That's about two o'clock. It takes us beyond the marsh—and the marsh is the only spot I'm much worried about."

"Don't lean too heavy on that. But this won't do. You've got to make twenty trips by horse at this rate to pull the accumulated dust out of Ophir. The odds against you get too damned heavy."

"This is the last one. Next trip we pile it all on the stage and make a run of it."

"There's your county fair for certain."

"We'll have a crowd on the ride. You and I. I'll get Rheinmiller to come through and ride back with us. We'll get another couple."

"Find the other couple willing to do it," said Bart Lennon. "That's your problem."

"Carrico and half-a-dozen troopers."

"Against Army regulations."

"To do it in the open, yes. But there's

nothing in the book to prevent his being at a certain place on the road at a certain time."

"Where'll you have him be—the marsh? You can't be that sure you're going to get hit there. It might be a long way off—then Carrico's squatted in the wrong place, no help to you."

"There's only two places we can be hit," said Rawson. "We go through the marsh by daylight, but there's cover enough there for an attack to be made. Beyond that it's open country and daylight all the way to Head of the Mountain—so we'll be let alone. That leaves us in trouble during the night run, somewhere between Head of the Mountain and the foot of the desert. There's your second place. We can work it out. Carrico will be in the marsh at the time we go through, hidden. If nothing happens to us, he can pull back into the hills and be beyond Lasswell's waiting for us during the night. He can follow us down the grade to the desert. That's all the protection we need."

"Will he do it?"

"I think so."

Lennon got up. He said, "Your ride tomorrow I don't like. If I don't see you at two o'clock, what am I to think?"

"Just keep on and forget about it. But I'll be there."

Lennon nodded and left the cabin. As he went down the street toward his cabin he

noticed the men in the blacksmith shop, but
passed by without stopping; and beyond
Easterline's Store he saw a single shadow
against the stable wall, too obscure to be
identified. After he had gone on, the shadow
moved away from the stable and skirted
Easterline's Store, the light of the store catching Tilson's narrow cheeks and sprung body.
Tilson reached the saloon, stepped inside
through the darkness to the rear door of the
saloon. He waited five minutes before von
Stern came in from the front.

"Rawson came out of Easterline's with a
couple loaded saddlebags. What's he doing?"

"Again?" said von Stern, and thought of it
a heavy moment. "That's dust he's carrying
by horse."

"All the way through?"

"No, to the stage beyond Lasswell's."

"You want something done?"

"Leave it alone. It's small stuff."

"Small or not—it's dust," said Tilson.

"He knows I know about it. If he's held up
he'd figure it came from me." Then he froze
into a long motionlessness, his glance pushing
into Tilson with a surprised farsighted expression. "And that's why he told me. By God,
laying a trap for me. No, leave that alone."

Tilson, leaving the saloon, crossed the creek
to his lean-to stable and stood within its
shelter a short time. He had his orders from
von Stern, yet he couldn't take his mind from

the saddlebags. *Little or big, dust is dust.* Why let it go by? This could be his own private deal, nobody the wiser.

He climbed the hill to the rim corral, brought down the calico, saddled it, and left it in the lean-to; then he crossed the creek and cruised along the street, to look through Rawson's window as he passed. Rawson was still inside. At the livery stable he turned against the wall, squatted in the thick shadows, and calmed himself for however long a wait he had to endure.

The rain had quit during the night, but the sky at five-thirty was so thick with heavy clouds that daylight had yet to break through. They climbed the gulch trail and rode immediately into the dense black of the timber.

He said, "You have a heavy coat? It'll rain again. Not a good day for a trip."

"I had to get out of camp."

A dismal dawn crept into the hills an hour later and he swung on the saddle to find her watching the mealy shadows with her pleased interest. She wore a plaid coat whose collar rose around her cheeks like the dark petals of a flower. The wet morning laid its film on her face, her eyes were sharp blue in this low light, and she had an expression about her eyes and mouth which always attracted him —a light gravity ready to break into smiling.

They came upon the burn and stopped a bit for the view, the valley below overhung by low clouds now spilling out rain. He swung wider in the saddle to watch her. "Big raindrop running down your cheek. You'd look beautiful crying."

"Never cry. That's weak nerves. I'm strong as a horse."

"I didn't say it right anyhow. Things show around the mouth, not on the eyes."

They rode on to the Portuguese Camp turn-off. They turned into the gulch, followed the winding trail for two miles and came upon a settlement of six cabins, all but two abandoned and stripped of their chimneys, squatted in the gravel piles and stumps of a once flourishing camp. Played out, there was nothing here now but Pearl Jeffroy and her husband. She stood in her doorway as they came up, a very dark woman past middle age in a nondescript dress; her face was smooth, her eyes alert and prying, her expression younger than her years. She said, in greatest pleasure, "Now, Evelyn, I just knew it. I can tell when somebody's comin' up that trail. I can just tell, long before I ever see 'em." A heavier rain began to break around them. "You come right in." Then she looked to Rawson. "I know you. You drive the stage." She passed her glance from Evelyn to Rawson and a warm suspicion began to delight her.

Rawson got down to help Evelyn from the saddle. He said, "I ought to be back by six. We could make it to Ophir by nine."

74

"I'll wait for you."

The brown woman said, "We'll fix a good supper," and her attention clung to Rawson as he went back to his saddle and rode back along the trail. Without looking to Evelyn, she asked. "Your man?"

"No."

"You want him?"

Evelyn laughed. "Why, Mrs. Jeffroy!"

PART
II
★★★★

Rawson spotted the man's tracks as soon as he came upon them for with him, as with any riding man, the day and its changes was a book of great interest, whose sometimes cryptic passages challenged his ability to understand them. The extra horse prints were mixed with those of Evelyn's and his own; the fact that they came this far and turned abruptly back was a warning he obeyed at once by pushing the horse into the timber. From that sheltered place he noted that the stranger's tracks moved up the trail at a walk and retreated at a run. That horse had small feet; small horse, maybe small man.

He could not be sure he was being trailed, but with the gold in the saddlebags, it was the only guess he could safely make. Probably the fellow had spotted him coming down from the Jeffroy house and wanted to draw back a distance to get set for a jump. He

pulled farther back into the trees and searched
for a passable way through them. The rain
made some racket and the wind rustled up
small echoes in the pine tops, these sounds
covering whatever noise his horse made.
Water sprayed him when he shoved aside the
overhanging pine branches; the horse flinched
as this cold stuff struck and, making no sense
of such blind progress, wheeled back toward
the trail. Rawson shoved it on. As he fell
downgrade at this slow gait he watched the
area to the left, and he passed each tree carefully, and swept each new vista, and moved
on with his nerves losing their slack.

Half an hour—a very long half-hour—
brought him to the main Ophir trail. Rain
mist dropped down until this silver haze
cloaked both trail and timber beyond a hundred feet and though the Portuguese Camp
turnoff was less than that distance to his left,
he couldn't see it. He thought: *What would I
do if I were that fellow!* He put himself into
the man's skin; he became a man hunting another man. That wasn't satisfactory; there
were too many variations. Going to the right,
he skirted the trail until he was well away
from the Portuguese Camp turnoff; then he
crossed the main trail quickly, swung left and
threaded the trees until he stood directly
across from the turnoff, looking along it for a
matter of a hundred feet.

He saw the man's tracks come down to the

main trail and swing into it, but here they made a churned pattern on the spongy ground and disappeared in the pines across the way. That meant nothing. The man now knew he'd been spotted. The surprise was gone. What would he do now—quit or drift on and try for a fresh surprise? Rawson, having himself to make a decision, gave his horse a sharp spur, and rushed over the main trail into the farther timber, muscles stiffened against a half-expected shot.

He relaxed with difficulty and moved forward, following the print of the man's horse in the soft forest humus. At the end of three hundred yards he was still skirting the trail and from that he judged the man meant to drift in this manner, out of sight yet commanding the trail for whatever might come along.

Before him as he so slowly cruised, the foot of Mulehide's east ridge appeared, making a kind of bluff against the trail, and presently he faced its side and saw it rise, timber continuing with it, to a commanding point. Here he stopped. The prints of the unknown man avoided the slope, seemed now to pass into the trail, apparently electing the easy route around the ridge foot. Yet, as he looked at that high ground, Rawson became uneasy with it.

His slicker was unbuttoned and his .44 hung close at hand in its holster. He reached

forward to pull the rifle from its saddle boot
and lay it across his lap. The more he studied
the bluff, the more definite its risk seemed;
but his restlessness rose up and he thought:
The hell with waiting, and angled deeper into
the timber to approach the ridge by a more
covered route.

The timber was still with him as he struck
the face of the ridge and began to climb, but
within fifty feet of the summit he was exposed
in a stand of young seedlings. He swung to
gain better shelter and, at that moment, the
sense of danger close by was as real as the
scent of a dead carcass. He bent far down in
the saddle, and kicked the horse into a run.
The shot's echo came before he got his heels
out of the horse's flank, the bullet's track
certainly wasn't far behind him, and the slug
slapped a tree close at hand. His horse had
urging enough and went up the rest of the
grade in long, grunting lunges, passing behind
a better screen of small trees.

He went out of the saddle, struck the
ground on his knees and crouched there an
instant, remembering how the shot had
sounded and from what quarter it had seemed
to come. He rose to slide through the small
pines until he had a view of the broken and
partially clear area directly ahead. At the far
side of this open space, in a similar thicket of
young pines and with his back to the drop-off
to the trail, the man somewhere lay waiting

for a second shot. The rain meanwhile had thickened and the light was too poor for decent seeing. Rawson took his short look and ran back to the horse. He retreated far enough into the timber to give himself protection, rode down the far side of the ridge, and worked his way through a rough gully to the trail.

He was now behind the man, and followed the trail back until he saw the small bluff, the young trees crowding its edge and the shape of a spotted horse zigzagging down the side of the bluff. The horse was plain in the muddy light, the runt-sized calico beast belonging to Tilson, and the man sat crouched and bobbing in the saddle. On that jumping target Rawson threw his bullet. The miss was what he expected, since his own horse shook him with its run. By the time he was ready for a second try, Tilson was in the shelter of the timber, rushing on.

Rawson came up, turned, and followed the man in. He saw Tilson's swaying back disappear behind the screening pines and he sent a whooping cry after the man. He was roused, he was careless, he wanted a kill. A branch caught him across the face, carried away his hat and shook him so hard on the saddle that, half out of it, he tightened the reins; the checked horse stumbled, went half down and threw Rawson clear.

He landed on one shoulder, feet high in the

air, the rifle still in his hand; momentum carried him onward and the muzzle of the rifle cracked him across the head and when he came to a stop he was on his hands and knees, looking directly at the rotten bark of a deadfall. He was stunned; he tasted blood and saw it dripping on his hand. He was shaking, not from the fall but from a continuing anger, and when he heard the pulpy echoes of Tilson's horse returning, he thought, *Thinks he's got a cripple*, and stood up from the shelter of the log. *If this muzzle's jammed with dirt*, he thought, *I'm in a hell of a fix*. Tilson and the calico were drifting in and out of his sight, past one tree, into a clear alley, past another tree. The man had his gun raised, waiting for a shot. Rawson had neither time to look at the muzzle of his own gun nor caution enough to care. He stepped aside as he took aim, saw the man's gun swing, and stepped aside again. He fired directly into the sound of the other man's gun, the two sounds making a single stairstep explosion. Afterwards, in furious disappointment, Rawson saw Tilson wheel and run.

It was late when Rawson reached Portuguese Camp, a single light from Mrs. Jeffroy's cabin towing him on. He got down, gave the door a drum with his knuckles. "It's Rawson," he said and led his horse to the rear shed and tied and unsaddled it. When he returned, Evelyn was at the doorway. "I knew you were in trouble somewhere," she said, and pulled him into the cabin.

She was dressed. The older woman, half ready for bed, had thrown on a wrap as florid as a thousand sun-sets, against which her plain brown face and pulled-back coarse grey hair made a considerable contrast. Her lively glance surveyed him, and darted to Evelyn. She said, "We had a nice supper, too. Well, some of it's left, and warm. Jeffroy's sleeping in the other cabin."

She clucked her tongue at the wetness of his upper body and the pools of water collecting around his soaked boots. "You'll need a strong dryin' out. There's no stove in the cabin where Jeffroy's sleepin'." Her eyes turned their innocence on Evelyn. "So then I'll sleep with Jeffroy. You sleep in the bed, Evelyn, and he can keep to the kitchen. That's modesty enough this far back in the hills. The goose-down quilt will make a mattress." She opened the door and as an afterthought she said, "There's a bottle of poor whiskey under the bed," and the narrowing gap of the doorway bracketed her laughing eyes.

Evelyn said, "We won't do the dishes tonight. Are you dry?"

He wore one of Jeffroy's shirts, his own steaming behind the stove; he stood barefooted with his back to the fire, the meal and the whiskey giving him a wonderful loose-

ness. He moved his boots farther from the fire.
"They'll be iron by morning."

"What happened to you?"

"Tilson was following us. I saw his tracks
and had a run for it but I never got him
cornered."

She said, "Did you suspect him?"

"I had him in my mind. Nothing sure—but
he was one of the men I put on the wrong
side of the ledger when I was thinking about
it in Portland."

"How many do you have in the ledger?"

"Not many. It's rough to suspect people."

She went into the front room and took the
top quilt from her bed and returned to spread
it on the kitchen floor. "You're tired enough to
be discouraged. It'll be better in the morning.
You know, I've never seen you discouraged
before."

"Until now," he said, "I never amounted to
enough to be discouraged."

"What are you now that you weren't before? I want to know. What was it that happened to you? It must have been in Portland."

"I thought too much." He shook his head.
"I sound like a damned fool. I'd like another
drink. Drink with me."

She got the bottle, half-filled his cup, and
measured herself a sparing drink. He circled
his finger through the air, prompting her. "A
little more in mine—and in yours. That stuff

kills the good and the bad alike. It's the bad I'd like to rub out now."

"What particular bad?" Her eyes were a deeper blue than indigo; the expression in them could have been anything he wanted to believe, anything in the whole run of things, top to bottom. She was von Stern's woman, she was nobody's woman. It was innocence he saw there, or the devil; he didn't know and never had known and though he wanted to know, it wasn't likely he'd ever find out. He drank the whiskey straight down and motioned again to her. "Don't sip at it. Let it slide all at once. That's what it's for."

She finished, mouth pressed tight, eyes closed, body shuddering. She laid the cup on the table and opened her eyes.

"Each time I think about you," he said, "I think the same thing. You're like that cut-glass bowl in the Klickitat Hotel. The light breaks against it and comes back brighter than before. The light goes in one color and comes back every color."

"Ah," she said, "you're reading things into me you want to read, making a mystery of nothing. Men do that more than women. That's why they get disappointed sooner than women. A husband expects too much. Then he finds it's not there, and he quits expecting anything."

"Your eyes are peaceful, but your mouth

isn't. You're some of this and some of that—
you're anything you want to be."

"I'm twenty-three and nothing you can't
understand. I ought to have fifty nice years
of living in me. If I'm lucky, maybe that's the
way it'll be. It's so uncertain. I wouldn't dare
hope for as much as you do. I expect less, but
I'll be much happier with it than you'll be."
The serenity was disturbed by a gathering discontent. "You talk about a woman's eyes and
mouth. Let me tell you something. When you
get interested in a woman, you'd better trust
what you see in her eyes, or her lips will taste
very bitter to you." She changed the subject.
"Who's on the wrong side of your ledger,
Hugh?"

He thought: *How do I tell her this—I ought
to tell her.* But he said, "Half the men in camp.
Hard to sort 'em out."

"You're lying to me."

"Yes," he said, "I'm lying."

"I wish you trusted me."

"It isn't that at all."

Then she was certain he had George von
Stern on the list and she was sorry enough for
him to cry; she wanted to reach out and touch
him, so acute was the feeling of pity. "I know
you've got some friends on that list. That's
why you don't want to say anything. Friendship's a way of being blind, Hugh. If any of
them are in this, they never were your
friends."

"I know."

"Don't let sympathy or loyalty, or anything like that, make you soft about it."

He rubbed his hands together in a slow circular motion. His head dropped and his hair, still damp, glittered against the lamplight. Jeffroy's shirt was much too small on him; it cramped his motions. He said, "Never killed a man. Driving stage, you think what you'd do if the thing came to that. But thinking and doing are two different things. Still, I know what I'll do."

"Do it well."

He looked up to her, interested rather than surprised. "When the bets go down," he said, "I believe a woman's tougher than a man."

She stood up swaying; she supported herself on the table and surprise quickened the laughter on her face. "You and your whiskey. Help me. Or can you?"

He rose from the wood box, where he had been sitting, to catch her arm. She moved uncertainly to the bed in the front room; she sat down and looked to him. "Oh, Hugh," she sighed and slowly dropped on her side, curling small. "It was a nice party. Who was it for?"

"You can't sleep that way."

"I'll take care of it." She put her hands together and slid them under her cheek; she turned her head to watch him with an oblique attention. Sweetness was thick around her mouth, but her eyes were alleys of darkness leading back into her mind and he saw nothing there but shadow. She was a contradiction.

"You're all right?"

"I hope so. I am, aren't I? Don't you do this to me again." Her expression became wary. "Why did you? You scheming?"

"No."

"Men do scheme."

"So do women."

"That's different. There's a purpose to it." She withdrew a hand from beneath her cheek and pointed to the kitchen. "You go. Blow out the light. Don't burn yourself on the stove."

He settled on his heels so that his face was at the level of her face. The tunneled expression grew more pronounced in her eyes. She shook her head. "You don't believe in me."

"When a bullet kills a man, it could kill a lot of other things it didn't mean to touch."

She was thinking: *That's as close as he'll come. It's not close enough, for if I tell him what I believe about George, he'll think I'm not faithful to anything.* She shut her eyes and saw no way out of the trap.

He said, "Do you hear?"

"I hear. You just do what you've got to do."

He laid both hands on the edge of the bed to steady himself. He looked long at her, giving himself away. When he swayed forward she drew a hand across her mouth as a gate. She shook her head and her eyes were as wide as they could become.

"Please," he said.

She moved her shoulders; the hand fell aside. "You ought not use so nice a voice on me. It's unscrupulous."

His mouth came in to shut off the rest of her talk. He kept his hands at the edge of the bed, he held back the rush of his feeling and kept himself gentle. Her head stirred, brushing her mouth across his mouth; he drew away before his wishes grew more demanding, as he knew they would. "That's the truth of the matter," he said.

"Damn you," she said, so mild, so far away from him, "now you're against me forever."

He rose, uncertain, reluctant to leave. He said, "I don't follow."

"Go away. Turn out the light."

He walked into the other room and whipped his hand over the lamp chimney. The stove's red compound eyes brightly watched him, the cabin shook to the rough wind and intermittent gusts of rain dashed against the outer wall. He settled on the quilt, hearing nothing from her. "Evelyn— undress and get under the blankets."

"I am. Will you be too hot there?"

"No."

He heard her small, whispering laughter. Then she drew a long breath. "It was nice."

He said, "Mrs. Jeffroy will be disappointed."

The rhythm of the storm swung him to sleep.

Rawson had just left Evelyn at her own cabin, the next day, when Carrico came into sight, striding forward. Rawson turned the horses into the stable and waited. He took Carrico's arm. "I want to talk to you."

Carrico walked with Rawson to the latter's cabin and sat in silence, none of his arched confidence about him, while Rawson lighted a fire. His delft blue eyes lacked their usual sparkle and, though his features were much too open and boyish to hold anything like a sullen expression, his shadowed spirit outwardly stained him with a discontented gloom.

Rawson stood at the stove, looking back. "Too much riding, Ad?"

Carrico shrugged his shoulders. "It's the futility of it—kicking these Indians from place to place for the damned greed of a few prospectors. Who eventually gets the gold? Von Stern and the storekeepers. So I am nothing better than von Stern's houseman riding around in brass buttons."

"It's one race against another, Ad. It's happened before—one pushes and one dies. Maybe someday there'll be some other race driving us over the cliff—and that will be justice to please you, when you see it from your place underneath the apple trees of heaven." He smiled at his next thought. "Seated beside some pretty woman."

"Is that my reputation?" asked Carrico, wistfully. "Am I so damned transparent?"

"A beautiful woman is the music you'll always dance to."

"Not anybody's beauty," protested Carrico. "Not every cheap little beast or lifted skirt hem. I'm not an entire fool." He sat forward in the chair, shoulders down, arms rested across his knees; and the onset of difficult thought made its creases across a forehead seldom broken by such lines.

Carrico, thought Rawson, *was a boy when he should long since have been a man.* "Ad, I'm going to take the dust through next trip. That's Tuesday morning."

Carrico took a moment to reshape his thoughts. "All the dust? Hell of a big package."

"I'll have Lennon, Rheinmiller, and maybe one other man riding with me. It might be enough—but if they laid the trap right, it might not be. I need your help. Can you give it?"

"What do you want?"

"I'll leave here the usual time, six in the morning. The place I expect trouble is in the marsh. Could you drift down from your camp before daylight with a half-a-dozen men very quietly and wait in the timber by Pennoyer's

93

until we arrive? Then follow us through the marsh?"

"Be careful. Always assume the enemy's trying to out-think you. Your attention has been drawn to the marsh—which might be a deliberate plan. Next time you may get hit elsewhere."

"The marsh is a perfect hiding spot."

"I'd not want to use it. It can be surrounded—and there I'd be, cut off until I had to come out or starve."

"A regiment couldn't surround it," said Rawson. "And ten regiments couldn't penetrate the place. If we're held up by daylight, that's the only logical spot. If it's to be at night, they might wait until we're beyond Lasswell's in the mountains. Follow us through the marsh with your detachment," said Rawson. "Then disappear, but meet us after dark, when we leave Lasswell's, and keep us company down the mountain to the desert. The rest is safe."

"Is there any other possible place of attack?"

"Not in Deer Valley by daylight. There's no cover. Not in the desert. No cover there either. No, it will be the marsh by daylight, or in the mountains after dark. The timing is important. You'll be at Pennoyer's when we get there—and at Head of the Mountain as soon as dark comes?"

"My word on it," said Carrico. "How's your leg?"

"Still lame."

"We're a pair of cripples," said Carrico ruefully. "Your leg and my spirits." He moved toward the door. "Perhaps I'm depressed because I have my orders for change of station. On the first of the month I report to Fort Whipple, Arizona."

Rawson shook his head. "I'll hate to see you go."

"We'll get drunk on that," promised Carrico. "I've told nobody else yet, so keep it confidential." He drew a deep breath. "It will be difficult to break it—to at least one other person."

Out on the street, he moved past Easterline's casually, but didn't look toward the store; he stepped into the stable for a moment, left it, and crossed to Evelyn's and knocked on the door. Her voice invited him in. As he opened the door and stepped through, he swung to see Beth Easterline cloaked against the weather, come from the store. Her glance caught him; he nodded, closed the door, and removed his forage cap before Evelyn.

She had been at work before the dummy; paused now, she watched him, smiling but critical. She shook her head. "Ad—Ad."

He colored, straightened, and dressed his shoulders as though he were at ease on the parade ground, hands and cap behind him. "I wish," he said, "you didn't think so poorly of me."

"I don't—I don't at all."

"Give me credit for knowing something about women's thoughts." He became easier and his blue eyes openly appreciated her. "Here I am, maybe a rascal in some respects, knowing you a good deal better than Rawson does, who is no rascal at all. I guess the rascals always do know women better."

"A man who makes a profession of women ought to learn something about them."

"There's your opinion of me. It jumped right out of you. You may be right. What I wanted to say was that I'd trust you completely, I'd never question anything about you. I wish Hugh knew as well as I do how honest you are. But he thinks about George—"

"What's the need of talking about it, Ad?" Then she changed her mind. "No, talk about it. Perhaps you can do me some good."

"Well, you want him."

She said restlessly: "Don't make it sound so naked, so predatory."

"Evelyn," he said in his kindest manner, "suppose a fight comes on and it turns out Hugh kills George—the man you liked very well once, and may still like as a friend. Then how would it be with you and Hugh?"

"I'm surprised you don't know the answer.

I think I could kill George myself, if he aimed at Hugh. Women don't split their loyalties like that."

He said, slowly, "Then you know George may be in this?"

"I've sensed it. Is Hugh certain?"

"I believe he is. There are only so many people in this camp who can be suspected. Evelyn—there's nothing left of George in your system? Nothing?" When she shook her head he shrugged his shoulders. "I wish Hugh knew it. I like you two very much."

"Can you think of anything I can do?"

"No," he said. "That's what people always do to each other—make confusion they can't clear up." He turned to the door and laid a hand on the latch, looking back with his half-smiling regret. "What I wished to discover was whether or not you knew George was involved. That's the way it looks. There'll be trouble, rather soon. I'm afraid of it."

He walked directly to the stable, got his horse and rode up the cemetery trail through the rain-sliced gloom. He made no pretense at subterfuge, but went directly to the cabin and stepped inside. Mrs. Easterline stood in the cold and empty place with a restless disfavor on her face. "You've been long enough." When he closed the door he could scarcely see her; she swung swiftly into his arms, her hands pulling his shoulders toward her with impatience. Presently he broke the kiss and removed his overcoat and spread it on the cabin's dirt floor. Settling on it, she held his arms and brought him with her; a great, relieved breath came out of her. "You needn't make such a game of going to Evelyn Harvey's."

"We ought to keep some caution. The more you and I get along with this, the more we ignore everybody else."

"Is that so wrong?"

"Not wrong—but the camp's not blind."

"Oh," she said, carelessly, "never mind the camp."

He slid his hand under her head, he felt her breath warm on his cheeks. Her features were vague before him, her hand was at his back. He said, "I wish I could see your face."

"It's here—it's yours—you can guess what's on it. Someday it will be an old woman's face, no use to anybody, wrinkled and dry. I'm glad you see me as I am now. I wish—I wish you'd leave a bruise, a scar, on my mouth. I really wish so. Then I'd have it. A memory, Ad."

He dropped his head to her mouth and they lay silent; yet the coldness of the cabin got into him, and his heart's warmth was less, and his mind stood apart from this scene and saw it too critically. It was her hand's insistence that broke the affair. He remembered other hands which had pressed, other eyes in which the upleap of raw fire had burned away the shadowed mystery he worshiped, other lips suddenly turned from tenderness to heat. He had come to another ending and the very moment he knew it his body lost something. She knew it, too, for she drew back her head.

"You're not comfortable?"

"It's all right."

A rising concern sharpened her voice until it was almost unpleasant to him. "What's wrong?"

He said: "I'm sad, Beth. I've got my transfer orders."

In the six o'clock darkness of a bad day, Rawson walked to the saloon, got a bottle and glass, and settled at a table. Von Stern joined him presently; this was as though nothing had happened between them, von Stern carrying on his affable part well. He said, "You want something to eat?" and waved a finger at the bar. He dipped his whiskey glass to Rawson; over the rim of the glass his eyes were direct and chilly. The barkeep brought two plates over and came back with cups and a coffeepot.

"Anything new?"

"No," said Rawson. "Not much."

"Riding around?"

"Took another trip with a pair of full saddlebags."

"I don't think that's wise."

"The last one," said Rawson.

"That's good," said von Stern and went at his meal. Evening's crowd moved into the saloon and the air grew warm and close with its smell of sweat, tobacco and wet wool. "My God," said von Stern, "I smell it in my sleep. It will be a good thing when I get away from it."

Rawson set back his plate, drank his coffee, and sat idle a moment, debating the wisdom of warning von Stern. He had decided to do so; now the thoughts were coming in again, the dampening layers of uncertainty, of wonder at his own judgment; and suddenly he grew disgusted with them. His original idea had come straight out of impulse. *Then go on with it.* "George, let's step into your back room."

Von Stern was too controlled a man to exhibit any definite reaction. "Certainly," he said, and rose and led the way. "Want a rye chaser for those beans?"

"No." Rawson worked on his pipe and lighted it. He swung half around the room, hands plunged into his pockets, and came about to confront von Stern. "Monday night I'll move all the dust from your safe and Easterline's over to mine. It goes out Tuesday morning."

"That's a heavy slug for one trip."

"I'll have four men riding shotgun in the coach."

"You still can be caught off balance. Might

be half-a-dozen men waiting for you around the wrong bend of the road. Might be ten. Might be a dozen."

"I don't think so. There could be three. There could be four. At a stretch, five. But that's the extent of the crowd, I'm certain."

"What else you certain of?" asked von Stern, and fell to work trimming a cigar.

"They can't make it, George."

"That's a flat statement," said von Stern. "Nobody can be so sure."

"I'll make another statement. They won't live through it."

"You had some luck, once. Don't lean on it." Von Stern lighted the cigar and came about, his full stare striking Rawson.

"I wish they wouldn't try. Some of these men I know."

Von Stern settled into the room's one chair, facing Rawson. He blew a great breath of smoke before him, and another, until the smoke was an uneasy screen through which he stared. Nothing more could happen to his face; it had settled as far as flesh or bone would let it. The change Rawson saw was a thing of small shadings coming from inside, a truculence, a contempt, a willful man's disposition fixing itself. *Now*, Rawson thought, *he understands what I'm telling him.*

"You damned fool," said von Stern, making no fuss with the words. "I like you. I did what I could to keep you out of it—but you've got to get into it. I never thought much of your brains. I don't now."

"All right, George. I made a mistake coming here."

"You did," said von Stern. "A sucker move for a greenhorn. You just can't play poker in fast company." He sat passive, his stare pushing against Rawson with its mud-dark strangeness. "As for Evelyn—you've got her, if it does you any good. Damn a man that breaks up another man's run and changes a woman's mind."

"Did she say that?"

"She came back from Portuguese Camp to give me my time. What did you do up there?"

"That will be all, George."

"I guess that's all we've got to say to each other," said von Stern.

"It was too much, George," said Rawson. "I'm not sorry for you any more." He waited a moment, curious to find in the big man's face the trace of some spirit which justified his old-time affection. He saw nothing. He had no regret and found none anywhere on George, and he left with the knowledge that friendship could die and leave nothing, not the least memory, behind.

Late Sunday night the inbound stage rolled before von Stern's, Lennon driving and Barney Rheinmiller riding beside him. From the coach stepped a single passenger, lowering his short and over-fat body carefully to the ground; it was Mulvey, overcoat thickening him to even more impossible dimensions, rifle crooked under an arm as though he were a hunter. The mail was thrown down, the reins tossed to the stable hostler. Rawson joined the three. "What you here for?" he asked Mulvey.

"To ride back with you fellows."

"You don't make the load any lighter."

"Just give me something to draw a bead on," said Mulvey, "and I'll pay my freight. I'm dry, I'm hungry, and these two crazy drivers ain't left me a solid bone."

They walked into von Stern's for a drink, and for beans and beef from the lunch counter. Lennon saw von Stern across the room and nodded; the cool nod he got back interested him. "George got a sore corn?"

Rawson nodded and, after eating, moved to his cabin with the three. He stoked the fire while the others settled themselves around the main room. Mulvey found a quart of whiskey in his coat and placed it on the table. "I don't drink mining-camp liquor if I can help it." He threw the coat in a corner; he noted the single bunk in the kitchen. "So I guess I sleep in my coat on the floor."

"Jake," said Rawson, "this may be rough. You're past such business. Shouldn't be along."

"Damn the pure arrogance of young men," said Mulvey, mildly. "You think the world's made just for you, and anybody past forty-five's supposed to shoot himself."

Rawson shook his head. "You're just talking. You shouldn't be in this party."

Lennon still had his mind on von Stern. "What's wrong with George?"

"He's the man," said Rawson. "And he knows I know it."

Lennon said, "How does he know you know it?"

"I talked to him last night."

Mulvey said, "You tipped it? For the love of sweet God, why?"

"To let him back out and call off the show-down."

Lennon said, "You still got some pity in your system for George."

"Not now. He had his warning. He won't call it off. There'll be a fight—you can count of it—and we've got to break that crowd for good. I want it ended. Don't want to be ducking bullets every trip the rest of the summer."

"Let's talk how we're going to do it," said Mulvey.

"Start Tuesday morning and go straight through. Carrico will meet us with six troopers at Pennoyer's and go through the marsh with us. Then he'll fade, but pick us up again beyond Lasswell's and follow us down the mountain to the desert. The rest is open country."

"That's good," said Mulvey, and rose. "Let's

have a drink." He scouted the kitchen for cups and came back to pour a round, filling his own cup three-quarters full. "That's for the quality of the driving I've put up with."

Rheinmiller said, "How many men goin' to shoot at us?"

"Miller, a stranger with Miller, and Tilson. That's all I'm certain of."

Lennon shook his head. "That's sendin' a boy after a man. They'll do better than three."

Mulvey said, "Von Stern knows Carrico's your friend. Might guess Carrico will help, mightn't he?"

"Yes."

"So he must have an ace buried. It'd help to know what it is."

After Monday's breakfast, the four of them began the chore of transferring the dust from Easterline's and von Stern's to Rawson's cabin. They laid the buckskin pokes on the table, one propped against another, each with its owner's tag tied to it.

"That's too much for one express box," said Rawson. "We couldn't lift it, all four of us."

He went to Easterline's and brought back a load of wooden boxes, with a hammer, a saw, and two pounds of small nails. It took the rest of the morning to rebuild the boxes, pack the pokes into them, and nail on the covers. In addition to the express box, they had five small boxes, each weighing better than a hundred pounds. Mulvey eased hir self into a chair and put his feet on a box. Lennon said, "That's no manners to show a young fortune."

"Never understood the stuff," said Mulvey, "and don't now. Who started the idea that gold was worth anything? It's all in the head."

"Because it's hard to get," said Lennon.

"I know things harder to get."

Stepping outside, Rawson saw Carrico coming down the zigzag trail on the south gulch wall. He waited for Carrico and when the lieutenant stabled the horse and walked forward, Rawson took his arm and walked with him. "The only thing I want to know," he said to Carrico, "is that you'll be at Pennoyer's when we get there."

"I'll leave here after dark tonight, go back and pick up the men and be at Pennoyer's before you arrive. Why don't I escort you straight through from here?"

"Nothing will happen short of Pennoyer's. It's too close to Ophir and there'd be no surprise. I want to catch these fellows off guard and end the thing."

"Who do you think it is, Hugh?"

"George."

"That's bad. A lot of things go down the chute."

"I wonder how many."

At six o'clock, the morning lights of camp glittered through rain and shadow and a dozen men stood on the street to watch the

coach go. This amused Lennon, he riding
shotgun guard beside Rawson. "Reminds me
of women filing past the coffin before the lid's
put on. Sin and death draws everybody;
they're closer to us than anything else. These
fellows expect to say they saw us the morning we started on our last ride." A misting
rain cloaked the camp as soon as they reached
the foot of the gulch and entered the short
valley whose ponds of rain water cast off a
low shining. The first hills were a muddy
streak ahead. "It could come quick," said
Lennon. "It could be on the first ridge."

"Too close to camp."

"Don't know how they'd lug away this
much in gold if they got it."

Mulvey's cursing came up from the coach.
It had been his idea to lash the boxes on the
seats against the side panels of the coach, to
provide added protection; gouged by their
sharp corners, he made his discontent known.
Half across the valley, a first light began to
silhouette the ridge ahead and when they got
to it, thirty minutes later, the road was a grey
tunnel through dripping black timber.

A small gust of wind ran over the treetops,
discharging sheets of bough-collected waters
upon them. Lennon wiped his face and,
catching sight of an obscure shadow, raised
his rifle on it until it faded behind. Little by
little, pines took independent shape. Two
hours out of Ophir the day moved in, heavy

mist breaking against the hills and threading through the timber. They came to the ridge crest and fell down the quick mud-greasy loops of the road into Deer Valley, reaching Pennoyer's before ten o'clock. Pennoyer had the new horses standing ready.

Rawson said, "Where's Carrico?"

"Not here. Supposed to be?"

Rawson and Lennon climbed down. Rheinmiller came out of the coach, shaking his head. "I don't like to be a passenger. Never know what the hell's going to happen."

It took Mulvey longer to reach the ground. "What we got to eat?"

"Pie and coffee," said Pennoyer.

"Carrico's not here yet," said Rawson.

Mulvey shrugged his shoulders. "Let's have the pie and coffee." They moved into the house.

Evelyn stood in her cabin's doorway to watch the stage go and was depressed by Rawson's failure to stop in for a moment with her. She returned to the back room to make breakfast and while eating she heard the voices of men rise on the street. Through the window she noticed a group leave the stable and cross the creek with a horse. She went to the doorway, presently catching a man hurrying toward the lower part of camp. "What was that?"

"Carrico's up there on the ridge, dead. Bullet in him."

She stood shocked. She thought, *Oh, no—not to him.* A light came on in the store, and Easterline appeared. Somebody walked from the stable to speak to him. He nodded his head and dropped it and then Evelyn heard Beth Easterline's voice rise from the back of the store. Easterline turned slowly and spoke to his wife, and faced the street again; his shoulders dropped, his head tipped, and he seemed to grow small. She heard nothing more from Beth Easterline.

Carrico, she remembered, had told her he would be helping Hugh on the trip; that was why he had left so late at night—and that was why he had been shot. She stepped to the back room and threw on her coat and tied a heavy shawl around her head. This was automatic, for not until she was in the street, hurrying toward the stable, did she catch up with her intentions. Hugh knew nothing of this and ought to know; by now the stage was half an hour on its way, but she could still catch him at Pennoyer's if she used the ridge trail.

The group had returned from the ridge with Ad's body. When she reached the stable she saw it lying in the darkness. She called to Borden Pendexter. "Please saddle my horse."

Somebody in the stable said, "Where's von Stern's horse?"

"He went out last night," said Pendexter.

"Never came back?"

"Not to here he didn't."

Somebody ran from the stable toward the saloon and a moment later Powell Bailey left the blacksmith shop and went in the same direction, walking faster than she had ever seen him walk. Pendexter brought out her horse and gave her a hand up. "Listen," he said, "be careful where you ride today. Where you going?"

She said, "Just a little way."

She waited until Powell Bailey came from the saloon. He waved his hand and shook his head at the men walking toward him. She heard him say, "No, he's gone." Easterline watched her from his doorway, face so grey, so old. She turned between stable and blacksmith shop, crossed the creek and took to the hill. She knew it would have been wiser if a man were going on this trip, but everything was shot through with suspicion and she didn't know anybody she could thoroughly trust.

"It's been two hours, straight up," said Rawson.

"Do any good for one of us to ride to Camp Wilson and see?" asked Lennon.

"That would make two more hours, coming and going," said Rawson. "No. Something's happened." He turned to Pennoyer. "Anybody been around here or through here, last night or early today?"

Pennoyer turned his head from side to side.

Mulvey said to Rawson, "Want to go back and wait till we get this straightened out?"

"No."

"Want to wait longer?" asked Mulvey.

"No."

The four stood loosely together, staring at the dim wall of trees at the end of the meadow. Steam rose from that dense, dank morass in fat spirals which flattened to mushroom-shaped caps at the top.

"Well," said Rheinmiller, "what the hell?"

Mulvey spoke to Rawson, "You're drivin'. You're the pigeon."

"Come on," said Rawson, and walked to the stage. He swung up and caught the reins from Pennoyer. Lennon settled beside him and put the rifle between his knees while he unbuttoned his coat to make the .44 on his hip more accessible. Rheinmiller stepped inside; the coach sagged low on one side as Mulvey's bulk bore down. "A fat man," said Mulvey, "sure carries a cross."

Rawson spoke the horses into a run over the short meadow. The first muddy shadows of the marsh timber closed around them and the road grew worse at once, the broken corduroy chunks sinking deeper into the black-bubbling mud when the coach weight came upon them. Rawson heard Mulvey say, "You take right, Barney—I'll take left."

Lennon's gun lay over his knees, muzzle forward, both hands quiet on it; he watched the forward bends of the road, swinging his body to catch a view around them. Rawson turned to his own rifle lying on top of the coach and reversed it for better seizing. He said quietly, "Fanny—Maude." No horse liked this place.

"Little chunk of ground ahead—that's their first chance," said Lennon. He slid to the far side of the seat and faced half-around; the muzzle of his rifle rose. They followed a long bend and passed into a slightly firmer area; Lennon, steadying himself, stood up and peered through the matchstick tangle of trees and shook his head and sat down. "Now," he said, "the center patch, where the trail goes off."

Rawson heard a sound in the distance and slowly swung his head to catch it flat on his eardrum. The coach dropped a full foot in the broken road and threw both men forward. "Maude, get over." His glance reached forward to the heart of the marsh which now came at them, to the semisolid island which occupied perhaps a quarter mile of space and out of which came the trail he had earlier explored. He called down to Mulvey and Rheinmiller. "Watch here," and he began his own close search. He felt Lennon's tightening nerves.

The coach rolled past the trail, and Lennon relaxed. "This is half of the damned thing —two miles more to go." Suddenly he swung and looked behind him, and let out a tremendous breath of wind. "That gave me a jolt."

"What?"

"Just the notion I hadn't looked behind me for half a minute."

The trees grew thick and healthy as they approached the margin of Deer Valley, making an excellent shelter for hiding men. One wheel went deep into a hole, tossing Lennon violently against Rawson; he righted himself as that side of the coach lurched upward. An old plank cracked and balls of mud flew back, spatting against both men, speckling their faces. Open country appeared ahead, seen as through a tunnel, and ten minutes later the coach left the marsh behind. Fay Miller's house stood ahead, no lights showing in the two o'clock grey, no horses around the place, no motion anywhere. Lennon put his gun on the place simply as a precaution as the stage ran by; then they were in the valley's clear stretch.

Lennon said quietly, "I am two hundred and fifty years old," and found himself a cigar.

Rawson buttoned his coat against the rain and set the relay to a steady run. The wind had dropped, the rain fell in leaking lethargy from slate clouds now becalmed on their easting run. He watched the land ahead, and the edge of timber against the hills. "Carrico's too much a campaigner to miss a skirmish. This sort of thing's his business."

"May be waiting at Head of the Mountain."

Rawson shook his head. "He missed the meeting place. Bad sign."

At five o'clock, the night sifting down its first layers of grey, Rawson sent the coach into Lasswell's yard at Head of the Mountain and let the horses come to their willing stop. He dropped the reins to Lasswell's oldest boy; he lowered himself over the wheel and stood a moment as the other three men gathered around him, hungry, road-shaken, and made edgy by a risk waited for and not yet come.

"We will have one hell of a long drink before supper," said Mulvey.

When they had eaten, the four men moved out into the yard again. "You want to wait here till daylight?" Mulvey asked.

"The night's as good for us as for them," said Rheinmiller. "Better. We'll make less of a target."

"You expect Carrico to be waitin' in the trees for us?"

Rawson shook his head, and Lennon permitted himself a rare moment of open disapproval. "Damn a man that won't keep his word."

Rawson said, "No question but we'll be hit. And we'll have no help. We could stop right here and not go on until we found Carrico.

But if he's failed us, there's a good reason. We might try to recruit half-a-dozen men around the hills to make a posse. We'd be wasting our time—men won't lay themselves open to trouble. They know what happened to Potter. I see no way of making this any better by waiting."

"All right, senator," said Lennon, "you've made your speech. Who's drivin' ?"

"My run," said Rheinmiller.

Rawson said, "I'll ride shotgun with you."

"Bart and me sit with the dust," said Mulvey. "I never was so poor-opinioned of anything as that stuff." He looked at the men around him, bending his head to see them well. "Anybody got any notions where the fun starts?"

"I'd guess within the first ten miles," said Rawson.

The coach groaned when they loaded themselves on. Lasswell's boy tossed the reins to Rheinmiller and he, always challenged by the hope of a record run down this mountain—broke the horses out of their standstill. "Yaaah, hup-hup-hup!"

"Slow down at the point of rocks," said Rawson. "That's the place Carrico's to meet us."

"But he won't."

"No. It went bad before now."

The road ran west over the meadow toward the wall of timber now blackened by the closing night. A mile distant, Elizabeth creek, crossing the valley foot at a slant, swung beside the road and moved with it into the beginning of the small canyon which was the gateway to Head of the Mountain; and creek and road slid into this natural water-level corridor, passing between rock walls forty feet high. Above these bluffs the mountains rose tier on tier, dripping black, shadow compounded on shadow. It was a four-mile passage to the break-off of the mountains.

They were a mile into this mountain alley when Rheinmiller pulled the relay to a walk, crossing a small pocket in the otherwise narrow place. Presently he stopped the coach. Mulvey called out, "What's up?"

"Carrico—if he's here," said Rawson. Then he added, "Not here. No use waiting."

Rheinmiller used his words as a whip and the relay yanked the coach on. From the lower distance of the canyon a sound began to form over the racket of coach wheels and traveling hoofs—the shuddering report of a falls—and the canyon lost its directness and worked to left and right, following the track of waters which, ten thousand years before, had cut this trench.

Rheinmiller called down to Mulvey and Lennon, "Quarter mile to the ford."

Rawson climbed from the seat to the top of the coach; he hooked one boot over the low guard railing which ran about the edge of the coach top, and braced his other foot inside the railing. He flattened on his stomach and laid his rifle stock at his cheek. The steady jouncing of the coach knocked his ribs around and scrubbed his pelvic bones hard against the wood underneath.

"If we're stopped, Barney, go over the side. They'll nick you if you try to bull through."

"They'll have to persuade me," said Rheinmiller.

There were no stars, no light whatever below the crowding mist, below the curdled opaqueness of pines and rocky bluff; the creek's broken water had no white reflection, the horses were shapeless ahead. They were making a small swing away from the creek and they were turning broadside into the ford, Rheinmiller holding the horses to a run. Beyond the ford the road made a hard twenty-foot climb to the chest of the south rim and entered timber. Rawson braced himself against the fall of the front wheels into the creek. He gripped the rifle and his chin slammed into its stock.

Leaders, swing, and wheelers hit the water with a long crash; the first violent bounce of the coach, hub deep in the creek, lifted Rawson and threw him to hands and knees—and a voice sailed out of the bluff's rim directly above.

"Hold in there—right there!"

Barney Rheinmiller let go his yell. "Hup-

hyaah!" The horses rushed toward the incline
at the creek's far side and the coach, now
athwart the creek, shook violently. A shot
broke above the rattle of harness and wheels,
and muzzle light bloomed and died against
the solid black. The off-lead horse, barely on
the incline, went down, its full weight dragging against the others, and the coach, thus
violently halted, slowly surged upward. The
other horses, in full panic, fought forward
and backward until the coach, swayed beyond
the center of its own gravity, capsized into the
yard-deep stream.

Rawson hung to the uppermost rail, rifle
gripped under his arm, and his feet dangled
in the current. He was wide-open for any
chance bullet ripping through the flimsy
coach paneling, and suddenly he released his
grip on the railing and dropped hip-deep in
the water. Rheinmiller was on all fours directly in front of him, half strangled as he fought
to rise. Rawson caught him at the arm, and
hauled him upright.

A full volley came from the bluff, orange
light points blooming again. A bullet whined
on the water, a bullet made a breathing sound
in passing through the coach panel, and inside
the coach Mulvey spoke a very gentle word.
Lennon's voice was louder. "Jake, hang onto
me."

"Get out of there," said Rawson.

The firing set in, scattered, steady, bearing

down. Rheinmiller squatted deep in the water. "Mulvey," he said "get out of there."

A bullet struck an iron tire with a whacking wallop, and a wild fragment of lead ticked Rawson's hat peak. Rheinmiller, still squatted, worked his way toward the far bank. Rawson spoke. "Jake, you want help?"

Lennon got out of the coach, slid over the canted top, and dropped against Rawson; he lost his footing and began to fall. Rawson caught and steadied him.

"He's sittin' in there," said Lennon.

"Got to get him out."

"He's sittin' dead."

Rawson ducked. He slid his feet across the rocks and through the current and reached the bank; he ran on ten yards and squatted, hearing Rheinmiller breathing, hearing Lennon come on. They crouched in the road at the base of the bluff and listened to the steady firing of the yonder guns.

"Revolver's soaked," said Rheinmiller. "We'll have to do it with rifles."

Rawson counted the rifle flashes he saw. "Seem to be four there. No—somebody's crawling down the road to the horses."

He saw nothing, but he heard the gritting of boots on the gravel near the water, directly across the way; he thought he heard more than one man. He murmured, "They'll get into that coach in a minute. Spread out. We'll wait a little while."

119

"Don't hit them horses," said Rheinmiller, and moved away. Rawson retreated until he struck the rock wall; he crawled along it, a naked target if these searching bullets found him. Over there in the black gut of the road a voice spoke, very small above the boiling racket of the creek on its shallow fording stones, and quickly afterward the gunfire ceased. Men were moving yonder; he saw nothing whatever but he caught the nearer murmur of more than one voice, and he turned his head to catch the sounds and place them. They were around the coach.

He raised his gun on the coach, and heard a voice sharply say, "Now." For a moment he failed to identify the sound which came after the word—the brisker grinding of some object on the rocks, the splashing of out-poured water, and the sharp fall of a heavy weight against the gravel. In that waiting space, with his eyes strained against the nothingness ahead, he thought he saw the coach shadow swell larger and change position. Then he knew that these men, all together, had heaved the coach back on its wheels. He fired low to miss the horses and to catch the men still in the water.

Lennon and Rheinmiller, from their own hiding places in the dark, followed suit, their guns beating the dark; a voice started to speak, out by the coach, and died on an incompleted word. The horses were in motion, the coach rattled across the ford, and the sharp bark of another man's voice got the animals into a run. He lifted his gun on a blind target, and didn't know whether he hit short or high. A splinter of rock jabbed his face. He dropped, crawled two yards, and heard another slug strike the cliff. The flash of the appearing gun across the water was somewhat to the left, in the trees at the rim of the bluff. He got to his knees and took a blind aim, waiting. Lennon, on his right, tried a shot and drew one from the opposite man; on that small stab of brightness, dead actually before he turned the muzzle of his gun. Rawson placed a shot, immediately rising to shift position. He got an answer.

The coach was at the top of the grade, in the timber. He rose, thinking to cross the creek, and remembered Rheinmiller and Lennon; if he got out there and made a noise, he'd be their target. He called, "Bart—Dutch, come in." Rheinmiller was suddenly at his side, having made no sound at all. Lennon's wet boots squealed near by.

"I'm going over there. Shoot high if you shoot."

"We'll all go over," said Rheinmiller.

"Wait till I cross." He moved to the water and pushed his boots softly along the rocks; the running stream rustled around his legs, louder to him than the crash of the coach had been. He went hip-deep into the center of the

creek and slid forward a foot at a time, braced
against the current's push; as soon as he
reached the far gravel he sank to one knee.
The sound of the holdup crew had shifted to
the right. A hand touched his shoulder from
behind and Rheinmiller murmured, "What
you hear?" In a moment Lennon's feet struck
him.

The unseen road went up its short grade to
the top of the bluff, turned to the right, and
ran along the rim, in and out of the crowding
timber. The coach was somewhere beyond
the bend of the road. Rawson touched both
Rheinmiller and Lennon and moved with the
rising road, they following. At the top of the
grade he heard the men more clearly, and
horses breathing. Somebody said, "Fay—
come on back." The voice was blanketed by
the creek's dashing sound, but there was
enough left to bring back the owner. That was
George.

The knowledge astonished Rawson. He had
underestimated von Stern, never thinking
him capable of doing this rough business himself; it was a streak of plain outlawry George
had kept hidden behind his manners, behind
the fresh shirt and neat clothes. *I'll never be
sure of my judgment of any man again*, Rawson thought. Lennon's finger poked him warn-
ingly in the right ribs and he held himself
still, gun half-lifted. Somebody came quickly
from the trees to the left of the road, crossed

not more than fifteen feet in front of them, and moved toward the coach.

Rawson fired, catching the blast of both his partners' guns as the same instinct moved them. The man gave out a short, shocked cry, and Rawson, running toward the shelter of the near-by trees, heard him fall. Rheinmiller and Lennon were close at hand, flattened against the pines.

"Turk!"

Nobody answered. Von Stern's voice came more clearly from the foreground. "Turk!" Horses began to move away through the timber and a firing started from the coach, striking the trees near Rawson. He slid half around a pine and sent a speculating shot forward; but the horses were running away and the voices, more freely calling back and forth, were at a greater distance.

"Now let's don't get separated," said Rheinmiller.

"That fellow dead, or possum?" said Lennon.

Rawson took half-a-dozen steps and touched the man's boots below. He pointed his rifle directly downward and kicked the boots and got no answer. He bent, found the man's arm, lifted it, let it go. "Not possum, Bart."

The three stepped forward along the road until the shadow of the coach began to rise before them. Rheinmiller moved ahead. Rawson turned to the coach and put his head through the door. Mulvey was still inside, his body lying full length on the floor and one arm thrust out. Rawson's face struck the man's cold fingers, the shock of it sending him backward. He said, "Goddammit," and then said, "Mulvey, you alive?" It had seemed that Muvey reached for him. He touched the hand and slid his arm forward. He heard Rheinmiller speak to the relay horses. "They didn't take the road," he heard Lennon say. "They went west." He rose to the coach step, explored seats and floor and came out.

Rheinmiller said, "Anything in there?"

"No—they took it."

"Pack animals," said Lennon. "I heard too much racket for five-six riders. Where's Mulvey?"

"Still in the coach."

Rheinmiller and Lennon drifted back and the three men stood together, chilled and thoughtful, listening to the last echoes of the horsemen die in the timber.

"They've got ten hours to run before good daylight," said Lennon.

"Pack string will slow 'em down," Rheinmiller pointed out.

"They won't run straight," said Rawson. "They'll hole up and pick their time. They've got a long way to go—six or seven hundred miles before they can sell that dust anywhere without getting into trouble."

"We can't do anything before daylight," said Rheinmiller, "and we need something to ride on."

"Better go back to Lasswell's."

It took a quarter hour to turn the coach. Rawson unhitched the orphan horse from the lead team and cast it loose, knowing it would follow. "I'll go ahead and roll that fellow off the road."

"I don't mind running over him," said Rheinmiller, "but the horses have better manners."

Rawson caught the coach as it went by, climbing beside Rheinmiller. Lennon rode inside with Mulvey. They crossed the ford, swung along the gorge and, less than an hour later, were in Lasswell's yard. The Lasswells, hearing them at a distance, were at the door, but they knew what this was and said nothing while Rawson jumped down to unhitch. He motioned Lasswell forward to take the horses and joined Rheinmiller and Lennon. The three brought Mulvey out of the coach.

"That potato cellar's a dry place," said Rheinmiller.

They laid him on the cellar floor, closed the door, and walked to the stagehouse. Mrs. Lasswell had the fire built up and the coffee-pot on.

"Where's the bay?" Lasswell asked.

"Dead in the creek."

"Best horse we had."

"Tell Mulvey," said Rheinmiller in an extremely soft tone.

Evelyn was familiar with the ridge trail as far as the big burn and knew that the side trail into Deer Valley was directly beyond. It seemed impossible to lose her way; but riding by day and riding by night were two different things, and though she watched the left side of the road for the Portuguese Camp trail—which she knew she had to pass—she was able to see nothing in this gloom, and after a time she wondered if she were riding in a circle. The night worked its tricks with her and when at last she reached the wide gap of the burn an enormous relief lightened her. Remembering Rawson's description of the country, she crossed the burn and hunted for an opening to the right.

Her horse found it. From this point onward she knew nothing of the country, but felt that any trail going down the mountain would soon or late strike the stageroad; once there she was certain she would know the direction to Pennoyer's. She had already discovered that time went slowly during the night and that distances stretched twice as long; so it seemed now as she followed the interminable windings of this faint thread through the pines, steadily descending. The ground was rain-slick and the horse picked its footing with caution, sometimes checking his forward motion to take short mincing side-wise steps around a bend.

Shortly, the smell of the encircling night grew ranker, the wind had a different sound, and the shadows were of another cast. The horse slipped and gave a small jump that took her half out of the saddle. It slipped a second time, it turned, struck its rump against a tree and emitted a trumpeting blast of wind. She hadn't straightened herself. She reached for the horn, missed it, and the next moment was thrown clear; she fell against the base of a snag, fell on a sharp limb, and the horse touched her with one foot as it made an almost complete circle. Heavy sucking sounds came up from its feet and a thick water splashed her; she heard the deepening labor of its breath, the quickening panic as it fought the bubbling mud into which it had slipped. Then—its pure terror infecting her—it emitted a clogged and strangling blast and fell still.

They ate breakfast before daylight and brought out three relay horses, two of which had once been used as saddle stock; the third was of unknown disposition. "He came from the desert," said Lasswell. On that horse Rawson put one of the saddles; the beast took the bit stolidly and laid back its ears when the headstall went over them. Rawson stepped into the saddle quickly and the horse, at a heel touch, broke into a brisk run. Rawson round-

127

ed him back to the yard. "You're both old men," he said to Rheinmiller and Lennon. "Take the saddles. I'll ride hackamore and bareback on this."

They returned to the cabin to pull the wet charges from their revolvers and reload with Lasswell's dry powder. They borrowed his caps, the remaining powder and rifle shells. They stepped out into the yard again.

A solemn young man, red-cheeked and round-eyed from a night ride, drifted into the cabin's lamplight. He said: "Mornin' folks," and climbed down. "My God, I'm hungry."

"Going anywhere?" asked Rheinmiller.

"The Dalles."

"In a hurry?"

"Like to get there," said the young man.

"A day or two's delay matter too much to you?"

"Well," said the young man, "I would like to get there sooner." The glittering directness of Rheinmiller's glance worked its way on him. "Might be a little delayed without much harm done. Why?"

"You've just lost a horse and saddle for that length of time," said Rheinmiller.

Rawson shook his head. "Only the saddle," and, walking to the young man's mount, he transferred saddle and bridle to the fresher relay horse waiting by. They were ready; they got into their overcoats and swung up to face a morning whose first light was the color of coffee brewed from old grounds. The road ran twenty yards down the meadow and disappeared; the mountains were still smudged shadows without the backdrop of a sky. Rawson looked down upon Mrs. Lasswell at the door. "Would you have anything to eat you could throw in a sack?"

She delayed, turning long enough to tell them her reluctance, and disappeared into the cabin. Lasswell said most gently, "You'll have to excuse the woman, boys. She's had a hard life."

The young man had been thinking about his gear. "Where do I get that saddle?"

"In Ophir," said Rheinmiller, "in a couple days."

Lennon stared at Rheinmiller a moment; and the creases of humor sprang around his eyes. "Maybe in a couple days—and maybe in Ophir."

Rawson said, "Can you drive four horses?"

"I can drive anything," said the young man.

"Drive the stage into Ophir. Lasswell can help you hitch and put Mulvey in."

"Who's Mulvey?"

"He was a man."

There was light enough at the ford when they reached it to search the waters. "I'm certain," said Rawson, "we hit one of those fellows when they were shoving the coach back on its wheels. I heard him grunt." But

129

they saw nothing; either the shot hadn't seriously hurt this unknown man or, if it had killed him, he had been washed well down the creek.

They found Turk lying at the bend of the road above the ford; of the three shots fired almost in unison in the blind black, one had registered—the bullet striking him under the left ear and passing out at about the same place on the right side. The night's rain soaked his clothes and bleached the skin of his face and he lay as a shabby, crooked shape on the earth with no more dignity about him than a dead animal.

"What was his name?" asked Lennon.

"Turk. Don't know his other name."

"Sort of a kid that didn't need another name," said Lennon. "Half a name was enough for all the business he had to do here."

"We hit somebody else," said Rawson. "Over there." He walked into the trees at the left of the road and made a futile search. The other two had gone to where the coach had been and when he joined them he saw both heels and hoof marks in the loosened mud, moving back and forth, interwoven, superimposed upon others until the small area was like a page of print blurred by a scrubbing hand. Lennon and Rheinmiller walked westward, each man trying to catch the story on the ground.

Rheinmiller said, "I can't tell, but I think

we got five riders ahead. And six pack horses."

"The pack horses," said Lennon, "mean they knew we'd be carryin' the whole jag. Somebody in Ophir had to figure that out."

"George did," said Rawson.

They got their horses and set out on the trail of the scrambled tracks. It led west a few hundred yards, reached a level section of the hills and looped around to parallel the gorge, returning eastward to Deer Valley; short of the valley, however, it retreated to deeper timber and by ten that morning, angling up the face of the ridge which overlooked the valley, it fell into the ridge trail. In that direction lay Ophir. Well along in the afternoon the prints took them to the burn and there started down the mountain toward the marsh.

"I'll be damned if I understand why," said Rheinmiller.

"These tracks will drop right out of sight and leave you talking to yourself."

"Just show me the tracks I can't follow."

The surcharged clouds were dense and sullen-colored; there had been no sign of sun all day and as they worked through the burn and reached the well-defined trail leading from ridge to valley the rain began in drops fat enough to indicate a heavy downpour. Daylight was withdrawing when they reached a fork and saw the prints swing right. Rawson pointed to the left-hand prong of the trail. "That comes out to the stage road at Miller's."

He led the way along the rough bottom slope of the ridge, in and out of smaller pines and thickening brush; the ground grew wetter beneath the horses, as though underlain by hidden springs. Perceptibly, in the space of a quarter mile the timber sickened, some trees showing death at the tops and others, long dead, standing stripped of needles and bark, a silver pallor upon them. The trail made a short turn, skirted a little island of land and ended without warning before a motionless, bilious pool of water. Beyond, other small islands rose, and the dead and dying timber, tilted or fallen, made a gaunt jungle as far as the eye reached.

Rheinmiller looked at it a long while, and studied the tracks which so definitely ended at the edge of the water. "They sure didn't ride into it. Got to be tracks somewhere."

"That's our little chore," said Rawson. "But look at it. If you put a thousand miners in here to hunt they'd all end up marooned on these islands shouting for help. When George wants to pick his time he can slip out and run in any direction. There's four sides to this thing and by the time we found the tracks they might be a week old."

"There's got to be a trail and there's got to be tracks," said Rheinmiller.

"Too late today to hunt," said Rawson.

The rain had thickened and wetness crept through his overcoat; the other two sat gloomy and thoughtful. "Don't relish sleeping out," said Lennon.

Rawson said "Let's circle around to Miller's house. It's a shelter."

By the time they got gack to the fork of the trail there was scarcely a hatful of light left in the sky; it was full dark when they came out upon the valley floor and sighted Miller's lightless cabin ahead. They drifted in, keeping the lean-to between themselves and the cabin. Rawson got down and moved forward. He tried the back door and stood aside a moment, listening. He called, "All right," and stepped inside. Presently Rheinmiller and Lennon came on. Rheinmiller had the sack of food.

"I could use a fire," said Lennon. "But it won't do. Let's try that grub."

They ate in the darkness and found drinking water in a bucket on the wash bench back of the cabin. When he had finished. Rawson turned to the door. "George never liked to be cold—and maybe they'll have a fire. I'll ride down the road and see if I can locate any sign of it."

"That's not too good," said Rheinmiller.

"If I see anything, I'll come back." Then he changed his mind. "No, if I see anything, I might try to get closer. Follow my tracks in the morning if I don't come back." He went to his horse, reached the road and, a hundred yards from the cabin, pressed into the march. There was no light at all.

The first shock of the accident passing,
Evelyn threw aside the feeling that she was
about to slide into the water and relaxed pressure of her hands and body against the earth,
somewhat disgusted by the panic which had
for that short while dominated her.

She sat up, catching the ache of her bruised
side, and slid forward until her foot touched
the yielding mud. Her immediate reaction
was to draw back and pull her feet beneath
her while a second, smaller fear went through
her. She turned and crawled forward but immediately she stopped and ran a hand along
the ground to establish some mark which
would identify this one place of which she
was certain. She touched a rotted stump and
moved on. She thought, *I can't stay here all
night,* and tried to remember from which direction the horse had brought her. It seemed
to be at her left, but she knew the horse had
made part of a turn before throwing her and
perhaps she was wrong. She crawled to the
right and again found mud; she retreated to
the stump to orient herself and now tried the
left. She went farther, and for a moment
thought she had found her way, but the
ground began to fill with water under her
hands and knees and, reaching out to either
side she felt the near-by mud.

The rain fell, soft and wet, and by morning
her clothes would be soaked through. It was

ten hours or perhaps more until she could find her way out, and she had begun to shiver.

She couldn't control the shaking of her body; she brought her arms across her chest and buried her hands under her armpits. Her face felt stiff, as though frozen under a thick pack of mud. Since she couldn't keep her interest on anything, she deliberately tried to make her mind blank. Some time afterward she ceased to shake and felt momentarily warm. The exertion tired her and she knew she'd be drained of all energy before day came. She tried to judge the passage of an hour. She cut the night into its other hours and could not imagine their ever ending. She moved restlessly; she grew too numb to move. She sat motionless and endured.

The thousand years crawled on and the stray creatures of the swamp, sensing daylight, began to stir; what she first saw was the blurred outline of a snag before her, then the corridors began to lead her vision farther back and the water around her darkly glistened. She rose, dull-minded, and put a hand on the near-by tree to support herself. The small chunk of land on which she stood seemed to be entirely surrounded by marsh, yet she knew the horse had crossed somewhere and she stepped around the place until she saw where the blackness of the water gave way to something green lying directly below the surface. She found a short stick and bent over to prod that place; the bottom was sticky but not as soft as the mud elsewhere. Beyond this green-cast gap, at six feet or more, stood another hummock and beyond that there seemed to be firm ground.

She drew on her courage and stepped forward into the water. As soon as she felt her shoe sink she withdrew and stood a moment in complete uncertainty. *But if I take one long step I can jump the rest of the way.* She laid her foot into the water again, without weight, gathered herself and took two rapid steps. She went to her ankles, grew afraid and rushed on so quickly that she fell full length on the solid ground before her. When she rose to look ahead she discovered that the way was no better than before, for water surrounded this miniature island as well. Then, completely disheartened, she thought she understood. The night-long rain had lifted the level of the marsh, drowning out what had been a poor path at best.

Somewhere in the distance there was a sound, but this she disregarded, long before having grown accustomed to other sounds which meant nothing. She thought she must be facing east for the light behind her seemed stronger; if that were true she was moving toward the Pennoyer meadow—and since the marsh was four miles deep and she had entered it at the halfway point, and certainly had traveled a mile within it, she ought not be more than a mile from safe shelter. The sound first heard came again, and held on. She stopped, turning her head to place it and, through the cluttered snags, she thought she saw a string of men and horses quartering over the marsh. She drew a long breath to cry out, and checked herself. *That's silly—I'm seeing things.* She began to tremble, half afraid of her mind, half hopeful. She closed her eyes, but the sound grew until she heard voices. She opened her eyes and saw the string clearly. *That's impossible—it's mud and water over there.* Yet the outfit approached as though on a solid trail. She bent forward, counting four men, and when she recognized the foremost rider she checked the forming cry and let her breath softly spill out; she dropped flat on a log; she watched the file go by forty feet distant and move on, George von Stern in the lead, Fay Miller and Tilson behind him, and a fourth man, whom she didn't know, at the end of the procession, using his voice to prod six pack horses, on each of which a box was lashed.

She remained until they faded into the shadows on her left. She heard the last murmuring of their voices and she thought, *There's a trail through this place. It's right ahead,* and she rose on the log and began to work her way forward, now fearful she might miss it; for the grey twilight, so slowly advancing, now came in rapidly.

Fifteen minutes or thereabouts after he entered the marsh, Rawson saw the fire; not a clear image of it but only a glow—and not even a distinct glow, but rather a disturbance in these shadows which were otherwise so unrelieved by black. The location of it was to his right and apparently a great deal deeper in the swamp, and as he rode forward it slightly strengthened. He went on another mile, which was half the distance through the drowned area, steadily checking the fire's origin until it lay directly over his right shoulder. Here he stopped, having reached that point in the road from which the side trail took off for its mysteriously incomplete run through the marsh. This was the only approach to the fire he knew about, yet he had no liking for it, remembering that it had brought him to a dead end on his earlier exploration. The horse, liking the prospect no better, turned slowly away. He brought it around again. The fire was the best compass he would ever have and, by daylight, would be gone. Without some such telltale point he might ride within fifty feet of those men and never see them.

He forced the horse into the trail which, for a short way, was easy enough to follow since it rested on the solid ground. There was not much of it and as soon as the horse felt the earth grow unstable it came to a determined halt, no amount of persuasion sending it on.

Rawson retreated a short distance, led the beast off the trail and tied it to a snag; then he took the rifle from its boot, checked the amount of loose ammunition he had in his pocket, and set forward afoot. Three steps onward, he remembered the lariat coiled to the saddle thong and went back for it, and set out again. He too felt the ground change beneath him, but there was a definite groove to mark the trail and by shuffling his feet occasionally he managed to trace its edges and to follow its increasingly tortuous progress from one hummock to another.

Sound came through the dark, rising from nothing with such suddeness that he wheeled at once and stepped behind a snag, his feet in water and slowly sinking until they struck the hard support of a root. A voice came in: "Let the horse have its head," and the hoofs splashed not far away. He looked into the glow and saw no shapes, and turned his head toward the darker quarter of the marsh, and heard the travelers quite close by. One shape came dimly in from the nothingness, followed by a second shape, both so near him he could have touched the horses; in another moment they were back of him, going toward the stage road. The speaker's voice seemed to be Tilson's; that of the second man, now complaining, wasn't familiar. "Don't go so damned fast."

Rawson stepped to the trail and moved on.

Now he had two men behind him and perhaps two or three in front of him. The light
was no longer directly ahead but toward the
right and the farther he followed the trail the
more it swung away. Perhaps the trail made
a long loop on its way to the fire, and certainly
the two riders must have come from the fire;
yet at the end of a quarter hour's creeping
progress he was farther from the glow than he
had been before, and at that point decided
he must have overshot another branch of the
trail. He turned and retraced his way until he
was about where he had been during the
passage of the riders. Judging from the glow,
this was the nearest point to the fire and he
began to walk back and forth in search of a
path which would cut across the marsh to it.
He discovered nothing and for a little while
he sat crouched and tried to unravel the
puzzle, meanwhile listening into the night.

No, he thought, *this trail must loop back*,
and he rose and went ahead. Once more the
glow swung behind him as he traveled, but
in a little while he felt the trail turning. It
made half a circle around a hummock and
bent again. His elbow scraped a log and his
knees struck another; he got down on his
haunches, sighting the low ground against the
glow and saw the silhouette of fallen timber
everywhere, the logs canted at crazy angles.
A wind, striking this rotten patch, had laid
everything flat. Through it the trail passed,

sometimes squeezing narrowly between logs and making such sharp turnabouts that he wondered how a horse could manage to make passage. He was again approaching the fire, the glow now acquiring a definite center. Over there, behind a partial screen of thin brush and stunted pines, there seemed to be an island of greater size standing above the muck, a hideout made secure by the waters around it and approached only by this trail. As he moved on, sliding through a log-crowded alley which shifted its direction every ten or fifteen feet, he began to catch an occasional glimpse of the fire itself through the tree spaces, a small fire made extraordinarily bright by the night's thickness. The trail pointed directly at it for a short time, came near enough to it that he finally saw two men lying about the blaze, and afterwards veered off; then he struck a log, chest high, and though he searched patiently for at least five minutes he could find no opening. Somewhere he had passed the proper turning and had reached this dead end.

He rose to a log and crept along it, directly toward the fire. The log led him downward into the water; he retreated a few feet, crossed to another log and followed this until it ran out, then dropped to the swampy ground, one hand hanging over the log for support. Ahead of him the capsized root system of a snag stood against the fire's glow, its dozen broken roots reaching out of the swamp like the desperate fingers of a sinking giant. He judged it to be ten feet away from him, across a strip of watered mud which might be as soft as mush, as deep as China. He didn't know what it was like, but he had been creeping through this place too long and he was too close to the fire to stop now.

He shifted gun and rope to one arm, stepped forward with a hand still hanging to the log; the mud was soft, yet not too soft. He released his grip on the log and stepped ahead and suddenly he was down to his knees in it; the fright chilled him and he bent his body and hauled at one foot with all the force he had and pulled it out and planted it ahead. He strained so hard his crotch hurt; he got his rear foot lifted, flung it forward, and swept his arm outward to catch the snag. He missed. He was below his knees in the mud and still sinking, and when he freed one leg he had to bend aside to bring it ahead. He couldn't get the other leg free; he pressed his mouth together, he gripped gun and rope, dumbly holding these things which were no good to him at the moment, and he reached for the snag and this time caught one of its roots. It snapped under pressure. He forced his body to a greater slant and got another grip on the root, and hung to it. With his weight off his legs he ceased to sink; he worked himself nearer the log, so low that his chest skimmed the mud. He got his knee on the solid ledge of ground which had supported the snag and hauled his other foot after him. Pushing himself around the snag's roots he now looked directly across a strip of dark mud and debris to a chunk of higher ground on which the fire burned. He saw the horses standing beyond it. Fay Miller squatted before it, his face turned full on. He saw von Stern rise from the flame and make an inspection of the surrounding shadows and ask Miller, "You hear that?"

"In this place," said Miller, "you can hear anything. Some of it's real and some of it's in your head. George, why'd you send Tilson and McLarney back to my cabin?"

"To pick up your extra grub. We're apt to be here awhile."

The fire's light illuminated the skeptical amusement on Miller's face. "Why'd you send those two? Why not me? You afraid I might cook up something while I was gone?"

"You might," said von Stern. "We've got enough dust here to turn any man's head."

"They can get ideas as well as me," said Miller. "They could crawl back here, stand off in those logs, and fix us fine with a pair of shots."

"Possible," said von Stern.

"You understood that when you sent 'em away. Now, then, George, let's have it."

"I believe," said von Stern, "we'll cut this party to two."

"Then it's just you and me to worry about each other."

"No," said von Stern. "You and I can't afford to quarrel. It won't take four to get out of the country, but it will take two."

"They're thinkin' the same thing."

Von Stern pointed beyond the fire. "They'll come back from that direction, won't they?"

"That's the mouth of the trail," pointed out Miller.

Von Stern looked down to the seated Miller. His voice was mild. "In a little while we'd better step away from the fire and wait. That all right with you, Fay?"

"I was waiting for you to suggest it," said Miller. "You're all right, George. I had my doubts—but you're all right."

The island on which the two stood was at least three feet above the swamp and its near edge came within fifty feet of the snag against which Rawson stood. Between snag and island lay a channel of water-covered mud which seemed impassable; no intervening hummock furnished him with a steppingstone and the snag had fallen parallel to the island, supplying him with no approach. He circled the root fan to its shadowed side, hooked an arm over the snag and moved along its diminishing trunk. He heard von Stern speak.

"Pretty soon we'd better let this fire die down."

"Not too much," said Miller. "That would

make 'em wonder. Tilson thinks pretty fast."

"Tilson's a damned fool."

"Man gets mighty smart when he's thinkin' of his skin."

Thirty feet down the length of the snag, Rawson stopped to search the surface of the mud. A fringe of brush along the margin of the island screened the fire so that the marsh cast off an oil-dark shadow; across this shadow a streak lay, like a hidden rib. He let his feet down into the mud and felt them sink and strike hard bottom; that was another log lying below the marsh surface. He balanced himself on it and moved forward. He touched a knot with his shoe and spent a rough moment teetering; he crouched to steady himself, and went on monkey fashion. The farther he traveled the deeper the log carried him until he was pushing foot-deep through the mud; a dead limb stuck up from the log and when he worked around it his searching boot found no more hard surface beneath. He had reached another dead end twenty feet from the island. He shook out the rope and tied an end to the dead limb and gave it a testing jerk. The limb held. He lowered himself into the mud, slowly sinking until he was beyond his hips. He rocked his weight up and down and seemed to drop no farther—that was bottom apparently, unless he struck a soft pocket along the way. Squaring himself around, he worked his legs against the rubbery resistance of the mud, half a foot at a time.

Von Stern said, "I've got to make some more coffee. Can't get the chill out of my bones."

"You been leadin' a soft life."

Rawson seemed to be pushing half the swamp before him and the effort cramped unused muscles somewhere below his hips. He stopped, at once beginning to sink, and knew he couldn't risk stopping again; there was a soft spot under him. He paid out the rope as he moved on, wondering if the snag's dead limb would hold against much pressure in the event he had to haul himself back. Far away he heard a pair of light, thin explosions, then two more, then one. He thought, *They ran into Rheinmiller and Lennon.* He knew the answer to that one—they were dead and wouldn't come back. His feet struck harder bottom and he rose with the solid shore of the island.

"Trouble there," said von Stern.

"Rawson must of been watchin' the cabin."

"I thought he might," said von Stern.

Rawson spread the brush before him, sliding sidewise through it. He dropped to one knee, looking directly over the flat center of the island to the fire, to von Stern's back, to Miller's tilted face. He lifted the gun, supporting one elbow on a cocked knee; then he dropped the rifle for a moment to wait out the trembling of his overused leg muscles and to settle his breathing.

"They caught up with us fast," said Miller. "I expected they would. But they won't get much closer."

"Rawson know anything about these trails?"

"Not much."

Rawson settled the rifle on his knee and aimed at von Stern's back. "George," he said, "you're covered. Turn around. Stand up, Fay."

Miller exploded as an overstrained spring, plunged both feet forward to scatter the fire, and immediately rolled away. Von Stern leaped aside and went to the ground in a flat dive. Rawson's bullet missed him.

The kicked-apart fire ceased to throw its light across the island; the hundred small eyes burning along the ground cast off thin, small beams. He lost sight of von Stern, the latter somewhere in the fringing brush at the island's far side, but Miller was still within sight, still rolling. He laid a shot on the man and heard a cry. He had registered a hit but he knew it wasn't serious, for Miller's words came up with their insolent intemperance. "George, this man's my meat—I'm goin' to kill him and skin him out." Then the temper died and his voice changed. "You shot me in the leg." He fell silent and Rawson, staring through the increased shadows, saw nothing of him; he had crawled beyond the light's reach. There was no sound from George.

Miller spoke again, a rising trouble in his tone. "Rawson, I've got to get something around this leg before I bleed dry. Here—I'll throw my gun at the fire."

It struck the ground near the fire and the fire coals leaped around it. Rawson turned his head from side to side, listening for motion from von Stern.

"Rawson," said Miller, "I've got to get over there where I can see. Can't wait. I'm out of this."

"Where's your rifle?" said Rawson. He retreated from the brush, moved to his right and crouched low to catch whatever moved against the dying light.

"Rifle's on my horse," said Miller. "Don't shoot at me—I'm crawlin' toward the fire."

Rawson shifted to the right again. He went on all fours, the brush screening him from the center of the island. He came to a log and settled against it.

"That all right, Rawson?" called Miller. "I'm going to move."

He caught the light breaking of a stick behind him and turned and saw a shadow grow up from the brush. The shadow swung thickened, swung again, and a gun's light was a lance thrust straight at him. The bullet struck hard by, whacking the log like a flat hand; he rolled over the log and threw two shots at the shadow, meanwhile hearing Fay Miller's boots pound the earth and Fay Miller's voice

148

rise high: "Get 'im, George—bust him!" The
man was on his feet, no bad leg, and rushing
forward; he fired when he reached the brush
and smashed through it and was a close high
shape when Rawson shot him; his feet carried
him as far as the log and there he fell.

Rawson looked beyond the log, saw nothing, and crawled around Miller, reaching and
moving beside the edge of the brush until he
was where Miller had been a few moments
before. Here he crouched, slid into the brush,
and waited. George had used Miller's rush to
shift position. This was the George he hadn't
known about, this tiger business coming
strangely out of a well-fed man who wore
white shirts and preferred the comforts of his
saloon.

He brought his rifle higher and laid a finger
on the trigger, gently swinging it; he was a
duck hunter waiting for a bird to break. He
listened and heard the small squealing of mud
under George's weight, softly begun, soon
stopped. George was foxy, George was waiting for him to turn careless. He sat still, but
the stillness was too much and he hated himself for squatting in the brush as the hunted
instead of the hunter, and suddenly he stood
up, took three quick steps and dropped.

Von Stern's rifle cracked in his ears, the
bullet skimming over. He rolled over and
brought his gun around. He saw another flash
in the brush, this bullet wider than the first.

149

He took his shot on it and he rose and moved forward and side-stepped and fired a second shot and saw von Stern's shadow rising. He put a third shot at the man; that one he knew went home; but he wondered why George hadn't done a better job. He pulled the trigger again and heard no report and, standing in his tracks, he saw von Stern go back to his knees and sink down, the brush breaking his fall. He walked forward, bent to catch von Stern's rifle, and threw it aside. "George," he said. "George."

It was the moment he had looked forward to with dread. This man once had been close to him and if friendship had any power it ought to leave something friendship had any power it ought to leave something behind— a memory of what the good days had been like, or the bitterness of knowing that no loyalty stood against time or change or the trickery of ideas. But nothing was left. He had been a foolish young man who had made friends too carelessly. Now he knew better; he wasn't a young man any more.

"Hugh," said a small voice far away. "Hugh, I can see you. Come and get me out of this."

He whirled and ran over the clear ground and through the brush to the black margin of the island. He said: "Where?"

"Here, on a log."

Twenty feet away, she sat straddled at the very end of a log, the weight of her shoulders sagged against her propped arms; the rising firelight showed a sleepwalking look on her face.

"Can you hang on?"

"I'm awfully tired, Hugh."

He couldn't reach her from this direction. He ran along the edge of the island until he found a narrow ridge moving into the darkness. The trail began here, carrying him farther from Evelyn until she was out of sight; but by now he had got accustomed to this indirection, and he watched the left side of the trail for the first sign of a break.

She dropped at the fire as soon as she reached it and lay half curled, hands stretched to the flames, eyes shut and her face so loose that she looked like some other woman. He moved over to the horses, uncinched a pair of saddles and came back with their blankets. He laid them against her, lifted her and rolled them beneath. She was a dead weight in his hands, murmuring through the onset of sleep. "Is there any water?"

He picked up a black coffee bucket capsized near the fire, moved to a pack lying on the ground, and discovered their grub supply. He shook enough coffee into the pot for a crowd and found his water in the marsh. She was asleep when he laid the bucket against the fire, everything about her loose except her hands: they lay toward the heat, doubled up,

as though she had to keep some part of her
body on guard. Her clothes steamed and little
patches of mud began to turn grey as they
dried; her shoes were solid cakes of mud, and
her clothes, arms and face were smeared with
it. He watched small ripples of expression
cross her face while she slept—the surface
waves of strange storms beneath. He let the
coffee boil hard for a good fifteen minutes
and set it aside; then cruised the island for
wood. He found a snag with a big dead limb
and when he broke off the limb it sent out a
sharp report which wakened her.

He brought coffee to her, holding the
bucket while she drank. "Oh, that's good. I
love that stuff—I love it, Hugh."

"How'd you get here?"

"I hate to tell you this. Carrico was killed
on the trail leaving town last night—no, the
night before . . . George left town before you
did, but you didn't know it. I wanted to tell
you, but I took the ridge trail and got in here.
I was out there on the log. I saw everything."

She made a little gesture with her shoulders
and settled on the ground, closing her eyes.
She slept; but though the fire warmed her on
one side, she was trembling and her face
seemed anxious. He dropped beside her,
drawing the blanket over; she stirred and put
her arms around him and he watched her
mouth smile. He bent his head, kissed her,
and lay still.

152

In the first break of morning he was wakened by a voice ringing roughly through the marsh; and he sat up to answer, recognizing Rheinmiller. He answered, but before he got to his feet he looked down at her and saw her waking; she was loose and warm and her smile made her lips smooth and when she opened her eyes she looked straight at him, seeking him out as though her thoughts had never left him during the night.

ABOUT THE AUTHOR

ERNEST HAYCOX was born in Portland, Oregon in 1899, and spent his boyhood in logging camps, shingle mills and on ranches, or wherever his father happened to be working at the time. After he had completed high school, he served with a National Guard unit on the Mexican Border, and later in France with the American Expeditionary Forces during World War I. He attended Reed College and was graduated from the University of Oregon, where he majored in journalism. After graduation he worked as a police-court reporter for the *Portland Oregonian*, and several years later left this job to concentrate on his writing career. A prolific author, Mr. Haycox wrote 24 novels and about 250 short stories. Many millions of copies of his books have been sold in all editions. A number of his books and stories were turned into memorable films and adapted for TV. He died in November, 1950.

More than any other author, Ernest Haycox revolutionized the Western story, bringing to recognized plot situations a deep and perceptive handling of people and a sheer writing skill that few have been able to equal.

SIGNET Brand Westerns for Your Library

*Prices slightly higher in Canada
